To Nancy,
&
Destanie

Blessings

Vanessa

[illegible]

2005

A Mother's Solution

by
Vanessa Collier

authorHOUSE™
1663 Liberty Drive, Suite 200
Bloomington, Indiana 47403
(800) 839-8640
www.AuthorHouse.com

This book is a work of fiction. People, places, events, and situations are the product of the author's imagination. Any resemblance to actual persons, living or dead, or historical events, is purely coincidental.

First published by AuthorHouse 06/02/05

ISBN: 1-4208-5203-5 (sc)

Library of Congress Control Number: 2005903986

Printed in the United States of America
Bloomington, Indiana

This book is printed on acid-free paper.

Prologue

Evelyn could not believe the turn of events in her life within the last eighteen months. Cruising unconsciously down Prospect Avenue, oblivious to everything, she fought her lack of concentration, bringing her attention back to the road. When and how had it all begun, who's fault was it, and why did it happen to her, she thought. Countless times she'd gone over these questions in her mind, knowing full well where to lay the blame. It seemed there were no other options, no one to count on, except, him.

She continued down the street, swinging a right at fourteenth, then, another right onto Euclid Avenue, which thankfully, wasn't too busy at the time. She couldn't have dealt with a lot of traffic with her hands shaking the way they were and all she needed to remember.

Sitting at the red light, staring expressionlessly at Playhouse Square, brought back pleasant memories. She'd seen countless plays there. An established tradition during the Christmas holidays, to dress her daughter Serrita in her prettiest outfit, have dinner at an exclusive restaurant, then see the nutcracker performed in all of its' splendor and dazzle.

She remembered Serrita's face, all aglow from the excitement of the evening's festivities. She could still see the beautiful black velvet dress she'd worn the last time they attended the show together. Her hair, expertly corn-rowed and adorned with beautiful silk ribbon. Her missing tooth gave her a cute but mischievous smile as she looked up at her from the candlelight dinner they enjoyed after the show.

Evelyn took out the sheet of paper, refreshing her memory of the address he'd given her, 689 East Ninth Street. A decent enough sense of direction told her she would need to go past Superior, closer to Lakeside. She rode two buildings away and began looking for a parking lot. Finding one on Ninth Street near the Rock N' Roll Hall of Fame, she joined the line of cars waiting to get into the parking garage.

Sitting there, waiting to get her ticket and find a space, the reality of her situation pressed her spirit downward, like a sinking ship, piercing the cold water, plunging quickly to the bottom of her tired soul. At this moment she needed her mama to say,

"Everythang'll work out, baby, you'll see. God'll make a way." Mama would say as she held her to her bosom, kissing her lovingly on her forehead, the way she so often did when Evelyn was a child. Her fractured heart need that right now like a broken arm needed a cast. Without it the erroneous healing process promised to leave her life crooked and deformed.

A gray-haired man in the car behind her leaned on his horn impatiently and waved Evelyn forward.

Mechanically she shifted the car into drive and did as she was ordered. From her position she had a good view of Lake Erie. On this cold, brilliantly clear, sunny day in December, the lake was a beautiful, bluish gray, with it's peeks etched in white. Along the shore, abandoned yachts happily bobbled up and down against the semi-frozen water in anticipation of the return of summer fun. The scene provided a beautiful feast for the eye, a calming affect, that would have under different circumstances given her warm and fussy feelings inside. But in the last few months she deliberately neglected to notice any beautiful works of God. She felt the conviction of her act slamming against her flesh like her father's old leather strap, beating her down unmercifully, with her rushing around trying earnestly to shield herself from the pain and damage.

Her life had been as close to picture perfect as any could be. Happily married to a man she adored, together, they had two beautiful children. Existing in a state of stagnant euphoria, when the rug was ever so rudely pulled out from under her. She'd been caught completely off guard, loosing her balance and slipping with her feet pointed straight up in the air, falling violently onto her back. Without a moments' notice everything changed.

The man behind her tooted his horn again for her to move the car forward. Bringing her abruptly back to reality, she pulled the car up to the attendant's window, "Fill up the upper levels first, ma'am." The attendant said pointing in the direction he wanted her to go. She removed the ticket from the automated dispenser and without thinking, moved forward.

Remembering all of the television car chases in parking garages she'd seen, she now wished that she were one of the actresses, with assured victory in an otherwise damned situation.

Finding an empty spot on the fourth level, she pulled in between the yellow lines and sat in thought for a few minutes.

"If this went off like he said it would, then I'll leave afterwards. Should I return to the car," she panicked as she thought. " Will the parking attendant be suspicious? My appearance will be different, so, he may not even notice me. Perhaps I should abandon the car altogether. Is the car worth me being discovered?" She thought uncomfortably. It was all too much for her to figure out. He hadn't gone over all of this with her. Evelyn shook her head in an attempt to clear it and pull herself together. She needed to be strong for her kids. She wept, thinking about Devon and Serrita.

Drying her red, swollen eyes with the sleeve of her coat she noticed a gray Buick sedan pulling slowly around the corner. Looking suspiciously at the driver, an elderly white man, she wondered,

"Is he somebody who has discovered my secret? He looks like an FBI man. Why is he looking at me like that? Get a grip, Evie." She reprimanded herself.

The driver of the car proceeded on not even noticing her. She opened the car door, looking down before she stepped out. The garage floor, freshly paved, covered in incessant blackness caused her heart to sink, feeling her-self simulating stepping into a black abyss.

Evelyn took the elevator down to the first floor, stepped out onto ninth-street and began walking slowly; searching for the address he'd given her. Cars honked their horns as traffic slowed down to a crawl due to a stalled bus. In a daze, she walked with no sense of direction as people walking, bumped into her, she didn't notice or even feel it.

Instead, she focused on an elderly couple sitting in their car, each looking straight ahead, neither saying a word to the other. She yearned for such a feeling of complacency.

Passing a small restaurant packed with people eating lunch she watched a couple sitting in the front booth holding hands, looking adoringly into each other's eyes, enjoying every minute of their time together. At another table sat three men, suited down, seemingly discussing business, oblivious to their surroundings. Waitresses moved quickly to accommodate all of the customers. Steam crept up from the bottom of the french- styled windows distorting their silhouettes, as she struggled to make out the strangers she wished were her. For a fleeting moment she thought of abandoning the plan Blake had carefully crafted. She yearned to just go inside, have an afternoon glass of wine, relax and forget it all. Instead, she gave her feet the order to move. She would persevere.

There it was, six eighty- nine, east Ninth Street. Standing directly in front of the building she began to sweat profusely in the middle of winter. Her throat closed. She gathered her coat up closer around her and tried to swallow as her head began to ache. The old brick building loomed monstrously in front of her. The double door, inlayed with antique mahogany was the entry to another life, a world unknown to her. There could be no turning back.

With shaking hands, she pulled on the brass handle and entered. Inside, she noted the musty smell and the outdated appearance of the lobby. She glanced over the directory even though he'd already given her directions and the room number, 216. She pushed the button and when the door opened, walked to the back of the empty elevator. The walls of the elevator were entirely covered in brass inset with ivory buttons numbering each floor. The maroon colored carpet looked worn and faded from the many feet that had rested upon it. The 'Carter', a grand place once upon a time, today just looked old and tired, the way she felt.

A bell signaled the elevator's arrival to the second floor. The door swung open and on the cheaply paneled wall straight ahead, was a sign pointing left, to 216. Her steps slow and unsteady, as if at any moment she'd loose her equilibrium and collapse. Standing nervously outside the door, she paused. The rapid beating of her heart shook her entire body. Before she allowed herself to think about it, she turned the handle of the door and stepped inside

Chapter One

Evelyn met her husband, Lamont while pursuing a nursing degree at Tuskegee University. An engineering student who caught her eye at a football game one hot Saturday afternoon in Alabama. Tall, lean and perfectly toned in his Tuskegee t-shirt and bell bottom jeans, he was fine. With a lightly misted Afro, perfectly shaped and coiffed around his head and face like a lion's mane, Evelyn, try as she might, could not take her eyes off him. She and her roommate, Lisa found seats a few rows away and she sat stupidly staring, hoping to herself, to be noticed by him.

In the middle of the second quarter, for the millionth time she looked again. Caught, he turned unexpectantly, having felt the heat from her stare. His gaze, strong and suggestive left little doubt about his thoughts. The shy, sheltered girl from Ohio experienced feelings she'd only heard about during late night girl talk behind the closed doors of her dorm room.

At halftime, completely oblivious to everyone and everything else around her, she had to meet him. She decided to kick her shyness to the curb and do what a sistah had to do. Just at that moment her crazy roommate, Lisa, broke her concentration,

"Evie, what are you lookin' at? I've been talking to you for the last ten minutes and you haven't heard a word I said,"she followed Evelyn's gaze,

"Ha-aay, he's a cutey pie," Lisa giggled.

"Don't talk so loud, Lee Lee," Evelyn blushed.

"Straight up, you trying to get with that ain't you. I know you, girl." Lisa said, taking a guarded glimpse in that direction,

"Be nice to me, I think I know him. He's Kevin's roommate," Lisa said devilishly.

"Kevin who?"

"Kevin from chemistry. Remember, I went over there to study that night. Uh huh, I guess that's what you could call it." Lisa always imagined herself having varied sexual encounters. However, that's all it really was; imagination." She was a coward at heart.

"Yeah, sure, Lee Lee. Stop looking back there, he's looking this way," Evelyn said, but to no avail.

"Damn, he's fine," Lisa, never the shy one, continued to gawk.

"Be quiet, he's looking. Now, get up, let's go get something to drink. And don't look that way when we leave." Evelyn said , rising from her seat on shaky legs. Lisa looked anyway. Kevin the roommate noticed Lisa and waved.

"Kevin," she yelled.

"Hey, Leese."

"You know him?" Evelyn whispered even though nobody could hear her over all the noise.

"Yeah, that's Kevin, are you listening at all? Remember, he came over to pick up my notes last Friday. He's cool. Oh, Oh okay, that is his roommate. I remember him now. Talkin'bout opportunity. Come on, Evie." Lisa commanded, taking Evelyn's arm as they were summoned over by a wave from Kevin.

The guys got up from their seats and headed in their direction. They met halfway in the center of the staircase connecting the stands, working Lisa and Evelyn over with their eyes.

Kevin and Lisa gave each other a friendly hug and began talking, leaving her to fake watching the halftime show, looking down at her shoes, running her hands through her hair, and folding her arms. She ran out of moves. The band pumped out "Brick House", as he shuffled his feet, trying to avoid direct eye contact. In desperation he turned his attention to the halftime show, staring blankly at the high steppers lining up to perform. Never having said a word to him, strangely she grew jealous of him looking at their perfect bodies and bright smiles. At long last Kevin introduced them,

"Oh, yea, this is my roommate, Lamont Hill. This is Lisa Givens and her roommate, right?"

"Hey, Lamont. Yea, this is my roommate, Evelyn." She discreetly winked at Evelyn.

"Hey," she replied simply, grasping for words which at the moment alluded her.

"Didn't you just go over? You pledged Delta, didn't you," Lamont asked, quickly picking up the conversation. She felt herself falling under the spell of his seductive voice and smile.

"You saw me go over?" she asked with a broadening grin.

"Yea,Yea. Right on. I noticed you. That was the tightest line I've ever seen."

"Thanks,"she said, unable to release him from her gaze.

"Man, we're going down to get something from the concession stand, yaw comin'?" Kevin asked.

"We'll catch up in a minute, bro." Lamont replied, then caught himself, not wanting to sound presumptuous.

"If that's okay with you, Evelyn. Is it okay?" he asked, a little unsure. He definitely wanted to have a lasting moment or two with her alone.

"Yes, it's okay," Evelyn answered shyly.

"Okay, girlfriend, see yaw later," Lisa said, nodding in silent approval.

Lamont looked around for a seat, realizing they were obstructing the flow of traffic on the staircase.

"Are you interested in staying for the second half,"

"Not really,"she replied, hoping for another suggestion that would include her.

"I'd like to talk to you, get to know you better. Do you wanna go some place where we can talk," he struggled not to appear forward.

"Well, sure. What do you have in mind,"

"Would you like to go to Auburn for a bite to eat,"

"Sounds great." she answered softly.

They walked down to the concession stand, found Lisa and Kevin, bade their farewells, and headed through the gate toward the campus. They walked in silence, hypnotized by anticipation. All he knew was, he had to be with her. She felt the same.

They reached Bethune Cookman dormitory, where his paint-chipped, sun bubbled, vinyl-topped Duster stood on its' last leg. He opened the passenger door for her to get in. She slid into the front seat thinking,

"He's the one." She didn't know how she knew, she just did.

"Let me just leave a note for my roomy. We're supposed to hang out tonight, however, my plans have changed," he winked. She felt a strange tickling sensation in the pit of her stomach as she watched him walk toward the door and disappear inside.

From that point on they were inseparable. He became her first and only lover. The fact that he came from Pennsylvania, located right next to Ohio, sweetened the pot even more.

Barely making it to graduation, the evidence of their love, her son Devon, a slightly noticeable bulge, pressing against the beautiful silk graduation dress her parents purchased for the ceremony. She remembered smiling, talking, and taking pictures with her family as she nervously contemplated how she would tell her parents she hadn't waited for marriage to have sex. Waiting was, up until that point at the very least an embellished facade.

"You ever heard of birth control?" her mother shouted later when she finally told her.

"Yes, ma'am," she murmured, her head hung low. The truth was, in her entire life her mother never told her how to not get pregnant. Keeping her head comfortably in the clouds, her mother found it easier to assume chastity where her girls were concerned.

Her mother remained silent for what seemed an eternity as she dropped catfish filets into hot grease on the stove, leaving Evelyn to squirm in her seat. She heard every chime and movement of the old grandfather clock, loudly vibrating off her twitching insides. Their plans to marry later meant zilch to parents as strict as hers. According to her family's way of thinking, revelations such as this called for a good butt whuppin'. Yet, she thought it preposterous that even her parents would consider whuppin' a twenty-one year old college graduate. Still, she put nothing past her mother, Ms. Ida Mae, as everyone, including her father called her.

"How many months are yaw?" Her mother sighed.

"Six," Evelyn mumbled.

"Speak up, gurl,"

"Six months, mame," this time louder.

"You been to the docta'," mama asked, lowering her voice so her father wouldn't hear the conversation.

"Yes, mama," she said, unable to look her mother in the eye.

"I knew the minute I saw dat bushy headed nigga, he spell't trouble. Yo' Daddy gon be 'spectin yaw to get married. Shit gon hit da' fan if dis' nigga tries to avoid doin' the right thang. Is his fam'ly don taught'im da diffrunce "'tween right n' wrong?"

"Yes, mame,"Evelyn had no clue what Lamont had been taught.

" So 'den yaw gettin' married, right," mama asked, as she nervously pleated her apron. Her hands, never idle, even when relaxing, her mother's hands remained busy.

"Yes, mama,"

Her mother got up, walked over to her, pressed her head to her bosom and kissed her forehead.

"Let me handle yo Daddy. We'll have a nice little ceremony in the backyard, it'll be okay. You ain't da furst 'n you won't be da las', hole yo head up, baby."

Evelyn remembered the succulent smell of the catfish her mother fried, lingering in the homely little house dress she wore. Caked up cornmeal lodged itself under her short fingernails, and as she hugged Evelyn, the crumbs fell lightly onto her face.

After that day, Ms. Ida cursed any and everybody out who talked about Evelyn behind her back.. To set family members straight she threatened to air their dirty laundry as well.

Evelyn's parents, Bill and Ida Mae Jackson left Barnesville, Georgia in 1948. In the scorching sun of red clay country, Ms. Ida Mae waited by the side of the road, for the Greyhound bus, a baby on one hip and two toddlers pulling at her dress tail. Clothes drenched in her sweat and stench, she was happy to wait with her screaming babies, she would've waited in a Tornado to escape the hatred of the Jim Crow south.

During the great, black, northern migration of the fifties, black families began the tradition of sharing. One relative, making it to the north made room in their already cramped quarters to accommodate another loved one who needed help getting out. In Cleveland, her father's brother, Uncle Sam offered them a second hand sleeper sofa, which they all piled happily onto.

With Uncle Sam's help, her father landed a job at the Chevrolet plant. Scrimping and saving every penny he made, he soon moved the family to a small apartment on the east side of Cleveland. Later her father's success as head foreman afforded them the three bedroom family home in the Forest Hill section of Cleveland, where her parents still lived today.

She told the story about how she and Lamont met to her children so many times, now they ran from her to avoid hearing it again. She smiled to herself as she closed out her thoughts and returned to her present task, preparing for guest who would be arriving within the hour.

"Lamont, bring the ice cream freezer from the basement for me, baby." Evelyn called down to the cellar. What began as a small get-together among friends escalated into a full-fledged dinner party. She knew this night would end like all the others whenever they partied with their friends. They would eat too much, drink too much and stay up too late. The good news was, her vacation began tomorrow. She listened as Lamont came up the stairs with the ice cream freezer, making sure he didn't over do it. She went over to the fridge and pulled out the creamy, vanilla liquid poured it into the center of the freezer then drug the rock salt into the kitchen from the mud room and sprinkled it down the sides.

They moved into the house four months ago to the day. With closing costs, selling their old home, moving, and trying to furnish the new place, it left no time or money for entertaining. Even a small dinner party was unaffordable until now. Finally, settling in and beating their expenses into submission, this had been their first extravagance.

"Ma, where do you want this table?" her son Devon asked.

"Right here sweety." she ran over and pointed to the corner of the room. Sitting there it would be accessible, yet not interrupt the flow of traffic. The perfect place for my deserts, she thought. Looking over the room for one final time, she felt satisfied about the placement.

Stepping back she admired her decorating abilities. The walls, painted a soft yellow, topped by a glazing process, were accented by the bold black and yellow print of her swag drapes. The red carpet with its' tiny, yellow, flowered print completed the decor perfectly. Beautiful Waterford dishes and stem ware graced the elegant, wooden table.

"Ma, Ma, this thing is heavy," Devon complained.

"You're not listening, I said to put it right here,"

"No, you're not paying attention, Ma. You looking at the room,"

"Whatever, Devon just do it."

"Watch your tone of voice when you talking to your mother, boy. Here, let me help you," Lamont appeared.

"No, I don't want you..." she began.

"Don't start." Lamont interrupted her.

Middle age, six feet and one-hundred eighty pounds, he appeared the picture of health. But, two years ago, looking and feeling tired, Evelyn made him go to the doctor. While lazily leafing through the latest edition of Ebony magazine, as they waited for Lamont to be called by the nurse, he grew short of breath and immediately had to be pulled into the exam room. There he was given oxygen, an EKG and the doctor started an intravenous line. Much to Evelyn's horror they phoned for an ambulance and when the paramedics arrived she learned that Lamont suffered from congestive heart failure.

Two days in intensive care, a cardiac cauterization revealed what the cardiologist explained to them as, a dilated cardiomyopathy. A virus Lamont may have contracted earlier, left him with a weakened heart muscle. She recalled the flu-like illness some three months before the incident. He'd been out from work almost five days. According to the doctor the condition was not unusual to middle aged African American men.

"Don't lift that, Lamont. You know you shouldn't be lifting that thing,"Evelyn warned. She felt like a nag, but couldn't help herself.

"Put a sock in it, gurl." He said, ignoring her warnings. The ringing phone distracted her.

"Hello? Haaay, Where are you guys? Okay, listen just come straight down Lee Road and make a right at Farnsleigh, okay, then turn right at the first street. That should be North Park. Kay, see yaw in a minute." She hung up the phone looking around for any last minute details she'd overlooked.

"Who was that?" Lamont asked.

"Mike and Lisa. They will be rounding the corner any minute. Ooow, let me get upstairs and get dressed. One of yaw answer the door for me," she said taking the stairs two at a time.

"While you're up there make your daughter come down here and help out, look after this food. Don't say nothing to me if the food burns up, I'm not responsible," Devon complained.

"She can't, she's got a date," Evelyn yelled down from the top landing, "listen, don't you worry about what Sissy is doing, you just make sure my food doesn't burn. Everything will pretty much look after itself with the oven being turned down so low." she replied.

Upstairs she mentally went over the menu again to ensure she remembered everything. Turkey and dressing, greens, potato salad, ham, fried chicken, a philly cream cheese jell-o mold, shrimp pasta salad, corn bread and for dessert, chocolate fudge cake and peach cobbler.

When she returned from her shower, Lamont had already served their first guests, Carol and Teddy a drink. Looking out the window, she could see Mike's Denali pulling into the driveway.

"'Bout time you gave the mirror a rest," Teddy teased.

"Sorry my brotha but some of us have to work harder at it than others, okay,"

"Listen my sistah, your natural beauty is always a welcomed guest at any party." he said, hugging her.

They'd met Teddy and Carol at a company Christmas party. Carol, a cute red head with shoulder length dreads, always wore the cutest African clothes.

Teddy reminded her of one of those African kings who posed in the cheap, velvet portraits of the seventies which everybody hung proudly in the living room of their first apartment, back in the day. With his sexy and muscular build, the only thing he lacked was a spear in his hand. Obsessed with the philosophy of Malcolm, quoting from his writings whenever the opportunity arose, he kept everybody grounded when the American way of life shrouded them in a false sense of security with it's big houses and shiny new cars.

"Haay, let's get this party started." Lisa said when Lamont opened the door for her and Mike. Mike handed Lamont their coats and headed straight for the bar. Lisa, dressed in black leather pants, a gold turtle-neck and black suede boots came over and kissed everybody on the cheek. Surprisingly, Lisa followed Evelyn back to Cleveland after graduation. Being the best friends that they were, it seemed natural that Lamont would introduce her to his best friend, Mike. The two wasted no time, a year later they were married.

"I smell them greens, gurl. What else you cook, no don't tell me I want to be surprised," Lisa said.

"All of your favorites darlin', I knew the first thing you'd be asking about would be the food." Evelyn said, instantly regretting the comment.

"Her favorite topic of conversation...food," Mike said sarcastically, handing Lisa her drink.

"I know you ain't tryin' ta talk." Lisa snarled.

"Now, now you two. Be nice," Evelyn said. Lisa's weight, a source of contention between her and Mike, because as Lisa put it, he hadn't done a damn thing but have an orgasm, she'd done all the work giving birth to their four boys. Plus, at Mike's insistence she was a stay at home mom, and having no relatives to stand in as sitters, she found herself, mostly stuck at home with the kids, eating. Still, the girl wore the hell out of a size fourteen, with her voluptuous curves and flawless skin kissed by the caramel flava sun.

"I want to see you have four kids and look this good after your body's been stretched, ripped, torn and ineptly sewn back together again, asshole." Lisa rolled her eyes at him. Their evening was getting off to a rough start, you could always count on Lisa to start some shit. Evelyn felt she needed to do something to lighten things up.

"Did you guys watch the debate last night?" Lamont asked, changing the subject.

"Man, if I was Bush I would never agree to put myself out there on front street like that, knowing that I had no debating skills whatsoever," Mike said. He pulled Lisa onto his lap as a gesture of apology.

"Kerry whooped his ass. He was on the debating team when he was in high school or college I think and from what I heard, was damn good at it. I liked the little smirk he had on his face whenever Bush thought he'd gotten the best of him. He went like this.. he had this kind of expression on his face, Yea, motho, ha, ha just wait 'til you finish talking bull, I got something fo'yo' ass." Carol imitated Kerry. She had a great talent for mocking people. Mocking everybody from Michael Jackson to Jay Leno, she provided a good source of entertainment.

"What I'm concerned about though is, this dude is a rather vague individual, you know what I mean? The only thing that I know about him is that he served in the Viet Nam war and his wife is the heir to the Heinz fortune. That doesn't really do anything for me, in terms of showing me a good foundation for his platform," Lamont said, taking a sip from his drink.

"Naw, but you know what, you must have missed the special they did on Kerry. His history was laid out very well in this documentary, I'm impressed. The media really did him wrong though, in my opinion,"Carol said.

"Well that's cause their arrogance leads them into areas they have no right to be in. Really what's going on is the media is electing people to office. The candidate's advisors decide just how the media should be manipulated, paying people to leak certain information, and hyping certain issues, feeding them directly to the media, they in turn take and run with it. Then, the media manipulates the people and the poor people, well they get screwed by an inanimate polling machine that's been rigged by whichever candidate has the most power and influence. It's all a conspiracy." Teddy smacked his leg to make his point.

"And, man they're trying to insinuate that Kerry's war record was falsified somehow, maybe he wasn't really a hero, I thought that was low, dishonoring a person that way who served his country, laying his life down that way." Lisa said.

"Still, that's more than I can say for Bush. At least Kerry was physically there, Bush's camp shouldn't have gone there cause he had some skeletons that he definitely needed to keep in the closet regarding his armed services record." Evelyn said. She got up and started a fire.

"Ain't that some shit, you know Bush's people put that out about Kerry. His ass couldn't even show up for reserve duty. I don't understand how a commander and chief can be the head of the armed services and with a straight face demand other people go to war. What do they have to offer in terms of experience. Experience gives you the wisdom you need to deal with delicate security matters in foreign countries and when you're creating strategies for war. I feel you need that wisdom to make those crucial calls, you have to have been there. Serving in the armed service prior to becoming president should be a prerequisite for the job," Lamont said.

"Okay, but I didn't hear yaw say that about Clinton, now did you? We, all of us overlooked the fact that he not only didn't he serve. He could've at least signed up for reserve duty and just skipped like Bush ," Mike challenged.

"Hell naw I didn't say nothing' about Clinton's armed services record, cause after Reagan I don't care about any of that shit, it seemed like a minor issue after having suffered under the Reagan administration, what an asshole he was, he and that anorexic wife of his, always talking 'bout Ronnie this and Ronnie that. The two of them wore the hell out of me with their tired ass racist politics, not giving a damn about the meat and potatoes sect of this country, the middle class," Teddy said bitterly.

"-Kay." Carol co-signed. Carol loved Teddy's polictics.

"Hey Uncle Teddy, Aunt Carol, hey Auntie Lee, Lee." Devon entered the room. He'd cleaned up well. Reeking of cologne, he bent down and kissed the women on the cheek.

"Whaz-up Uncle Mikey Mike," he and Mike clasped hands for a power shake.

"You got it young-blood," he smiled and patted Devon on the back.

"Naw you da one. I see you pushing that Denali out there. That is tight. When can a brotha catch a ride in that?"

"Listen, you, me and your Dad have tickets to the Brown's game Sunday, right? Kay, you driving the Denali,"Mike said.

"You kiddin' me, right. Awesome, buddy," Devon said.

"You still doing good in school?" Mike asked.

"Dad run it down fo'em. Dean's list again, don't hate ya'aw, I know I'm puttin' a hurtin' on ya'aw, Uncle Mike. I can't let da old cats out do me, ya 'undistand," he teased,

"Uncle Teddy. Come up and take a look at this new piece of artwork I got at the black arts festival in Atlanta this summer. It's Malcolm and Mandela together."

"That's right they did meet didn't they."Teddy reflected as they headed for Devon's room. Everybody followed. Evelyn thought it would be the perfect time to get the food on the table and move the party forward.

Just then, the door bell rang. When she answered it, she felt sorely disappointed to see Brenda and Carl standing in the doorway with the phoniest of smiles plastered on their fake ass faces.

Chapter Two

With the arrival of the other guests, a few more apple martinis, some good food and stimulating conversation, the party turned into a raving success. Sly and the Family Stone's, Thank You played on the CD player as everybody waved their hands in the air, chair dancing between bites of food, and thinking about how well they'd partied during their youth . Evelyn had a buzz on but got up to do the dishes before it got the best of her. Carol and Lisa immediately followed to help.

"No you don't. Cause I ain't doing no dishes when I come to your house, sit down and flirt with yo husbands, make'em think you might give'em some tonight." she laughed, hurrying so she could return to her guests. Lamont came into the kitchen behind her with a stack of dirty plates, helping to clear the table.

Even though she didn't like for her friends to help with the dishes, it pissed her off that Brenda hadn't even offered to help. The heifa was the kind of person who never returned invites and never offered to help her hostess out. She sat on her ass like a damn queen, monopolizing the conversation, as if what she had to say, would somehow prove relevant. The inside of her head was as empty as a garbage can, laying strewn across the grass on the day of collection. Her days were spent fluffing up the satin pillows on her Humphrey Bogart inspired, four poster, leather bed, which she draped in a two thousand dollar duvet. During parties she passed the time by making frequent trips to the restroom. If the truth be told she used these numerous trips to the restroom as an opportunity first, to snoop and secondly, to steal leftover drugs from the medicine cabinet. Evelyn really shouldn't have invited her and Carl but Lamont insisted, he and Carl were co-workers.

The "Dog Catcher" by the Funkadelics, began to spin. Everybody got up feeling comfortable doing a dance they remembered and didn't look ridiculous doing. The party was pumped. The men, feeling a little mellow got down and dirty with it.

" Ha-ay that's the jam," Lisa said, backing it up for Mike. Teddy started in with Carol,

"Don't even try it, you better back up off me now. Why can't you dance normal like everybody else, man," Carol laughed, pushing Teddy away. Everytime Teddy got drunk he wanted to do the x-rated version of the dog and Evelyn wondered how the stuffed shirts at the university where he worked as a tenured chemistry professor would feel if they could see him now.

"Baby, back it up fo' me, I'm ready to get it on," he slurred his words, becoming aroused by Carol's perfectly formed behind, made even more pronounced by her tiny waist.

" Negro, you better behave yourself in public, remember I'm yo baby's Mama, show yo baby's mama some respect,"Carol played him. Overtly sexual at home but in public her modesty annoyed Teddy.

"What the hell does that mean, what's that got to do with anything. And I know you didn't just use that word. You know how I hate that word, woman. It is the embodiment of an oppressive philosophy, whose origins stem from the old white boy network of European descent and is perpetuated by the Jim Crow hook up of these here United States." Teddy stumbled over his own feet.

" Sit yo' ass down before you embarrass yourself." She grabbed him and made him sit down. A statement like that usually led to a lengthy, militant speech about brainwashed blacks in America. Carol saved them all, by dragging Teddy over to the sofa and snuggling by the fire.

"Oh yea, this'll work, yea this is much better." Teddy murmurred.

Lisa and Mike retreated to a dark corner of the room and Evelyn knew heavy petting would follow. With four boys, all under the age of fifteen they found little time to spend alone. Barry White's, No More Tears, came on next. All the couples found themselves a spot on the plush, white, shag carpet near the fire. The room quieted down as the couples withdrew into themselves. Evelyn refreshed everyone's drink, arranged the desert and lit some candles, finally settling down next to her man and as soon as she did,

"Ma, Ma, Ma." The words came floating intrusively down the stairs. Evelyn, enjoying snuggling time with Lamont, was annoyed.

"Go see what she want, baby." Lamont sighed. With the moment spoiled, he released Evelyn from his embrace, and with his release, she imagined the little droplets of passion evaporated into thin air.

Evelyn ascended the stairs, her mind still on Lamont. She could hear her daughter Serrita, who they nicknamed, Sissy, rummaging through her closet.

"Ma, please can I borrow your red suede boots? I'll bring them back and put them right where I found them, I promise,"Sissy turned around in circles looking for the boots.

"Little girl, just turn to your left. Now, look straight ahead," Evelyn leaned against the archway to her spacious walk-in closet with her arms folded, smiling adoringly at her daughter.

"Thanks ma,"

"Don't let me have to ask you for my boots back, now." Evelyn sat down on Sissy's bed, watching her put the final touches of make-up on her flawless, caramel face. The black mini skirt, black turtleneck and red leather jacket were perfectly accessorized by the red suede boots.

"So, who did you say this guy was again, baby?" Evelyn inquired, cleaning crumbs from underneath her fingernails. She'd treat herself tomorrow and have her nails done.

Only moderately interested, still, she knew Lamont would hold her accountable for the young man's credentials. She took in the fact that Sissy didn't make direct eye contact with her when questioned about the young man. She couldn't help but be suspicious when her kids avoided looking at her that way, call it intuition.

"Ma, well he's somebody I met at the mall. I want you to like him 'cause well I think he's nice," she hated it when her kids stumbled over their words that way. She always suspected that somewhere between the words, were hidden lies or some type of cover-up.

"I'll like him if he's worthy of being liked. Still, I want you to have a lot of friends, not just one, because if you're seeing just one person the pressure for sex is more likely,"

"Lady, don't worry, I got my back." She heard the doorbell ring. Sissy darted out of the bathroom, almost tripping over a shoe she'd left in the middle of the floor.

"Ma, please don't let Daddy answer the door, you know how he is,"

"Alright, alright, I'm going," Evelyn knew she'd never make it in time anyway and so, she wasn't about to put herself out.

"Ma," Sissy pleaded.

"Oops, sorry, too late." Evelyn teased, running behind her, squinting to see the mystery man, whose greatest accomplishment so far was, hanging out at the mall.

The mysterious date waited behind the partially opened front door, or either Lamont made him wait there. As she rounded the corner of the landing, positioning herself for a good look, but remaining incognito. Her humerous and mellow mood changed abruptly when she finally did see him. One minute she was smiling and within seconds her smile, wiped clean away, as if it had been hi-jacked.

The young man, already having rubbed Lamont the wrong way, didn't have manners enough to avoid the confrontational exchange of words the two were having. A terrible sinking feeling groped her in the stomach and she didn't know why. She could see why Sissy was attracted to him. He was tall, with a smooth chocolate complexion, he wore a red "du-rag" wrapped tightly around his head. A single silver earring dangled defiantly from his left ear. From his wicked facial expression, to the suggestive body language and the abrupt manner in which he angrily flung his words at you, when he spoke, it felt as if you'd been whipped, or at the very least disrespected. His picture for sure would be found in Webster's Dictionary, next to the word, 'trouble'. Evelyn smelled it, the trouble that is. It was as strong as the pungent odor from a provoked skunk, fear of being sprayed should have caused them all to turn and run.

Making a slow dessent down the staircase, she listened intently to the conversation between him and Lamont, which had now turned rancid.

"Yeah, dat's right. I came ta' pick her up, she gon' ride wit' me tonight, dawg,"

"Ride.. where?" Lamont looked at the young man over the rim of his glasses, and then said, "When my daughter leaves the house with a young man, I assume she has a destination in mind, and the name is Mr. Hill,"

"Desti'nation?" The young man pretended not to understand.

"Yes, you know, she knows where the hell they're going, where they will end up, a movie, a play, a dance, comprende'. Is this guy for real?" Lamont said to Mike.

"What's up, bro?" Mike asked, eyeing the young man. Evelyn stood in the middle of all the action, with Sissy right on her heels.

"I'm not sure if he speaks English, I asked him a simple question. He saunters in here to pick up my daughter and he's telling me he don't know where they're going. He doesn't even have the descency to make something up. I think he just got smart with me. Is it me, or should I ask this negro outta my house." Lamont said. Nostrils flaring, he grew increasingly agitated. The young man rubbed his go-tee with abandon, standing his ground, assured he'd be victorious in the end.

"Is this Sissy's date," Evelyn tried to salvage the situation for Sissy's sake,

"Yes, Ma, this is Brandon," she turned to her father, "Daddy, please,"

"Sup'," Brandon said. His speech, habitually, intentionally, slow and sensual, was inappropiate. Evelyn suspected that it charmed many older women but she found herself disgusted by it. She ignored his extended hand. With the tension in the room building, word by word, the stack becoming taller and taller, her imbalanced anxiety threatened to topple over.

"Wait man, talk to her about it later, Sissy's got good sense. Don't embarrass her now," Mike said to Lamont.

"Sissy, I need to know exactly where you're going or you don't get out of this house. I'm your father and you are my responsibility, so before you leave here you need to tell me where you're going. He's not my child, you are,"Lamont warned her.

"Ma, please do something with him," she sounded like a spoiled brat.

"Sorry, but I think that's a reasonable request, girlfriend." Evelyn could still hear Lamont rambling on behind her. Sorry to admit it, she knew that some of his behavior came from the wine he drank earlier that evening. It was making it's presence felt like an unwelcome relative at a family reunion, hanging around indefinitely and unwanted. Still, she admitted to herself, there was something quite disturbing about Brandon and in this particular case the term premonition would prove adequate.

"Would you like it if he came to pick up your daughter? You open the door and Tupac, in the flesh is waiting to take your little girl out for the evening. Don't get me wrong, Tupac is cool with me as long as he remains in the lyrics of a rap song, but I sure as hell don't want his ass comin' here to pick up my daughter, you feel me."Lamont reasoned.

Suddenly, out of nowhere, in the midst of all the confusion, as her mother's treasured grandfather clock chimed in the hour, with Teddy Pendagrass singing softly in the background,

Turn out the lights, Evelyn heard it,

"Let's ride, baby." Brandon ordered her, ending all the confusion. All conversation ceased, turning their attention to Sissy, anticipating her response. Sissy's arm brushed her stomach as she turned to Brandon. Evelyn's heart pumped faster as Sissy and Brandon co-joined themselves in a gaze that told the story. Sissy never looked back as she slowly sauntered over to him, unconsciously moving her hips in a way, only familiar to him. His eyes impertinently caressed her suggestive sway. Clearing her throat, hoping the noise would hide the implication, yet, silently recognizing the relationship for what it was, a sexual one. She tried to dismiss the thought from her mind, but couldn't. Images of her baby flashed before her eyes in various sexual positions with this character choked her. As she spoke, her voice sounded distant and frightened,

"Don't be late, honey. Be safe." her voice trailed after them. Sissy was already on her way to the car, hurrying before her parents tried to alter her plans. Standing behind the closed screen door, he waited to oppose any opposition, as if he had the right. For a second or two, he and Evelyn exchanged a confrontational glance, each silently declaring war. His sneer of a smile turned into a snarl as he silently formed the word, "Bitch". It felt a dream as she watched his mouth push it out.

Evelyn desreetly peered from behind the curtains of her front door while replaying the scene in her mind. Perhaps she'd misunderstood what he said, after all he hadn't actually said anything she could hear. Picturing his mouth, moving, she saw the word silently come out, plop, like the sudden birth of satan's baby, and in her heart she admitted, Sissy was in trouble.

It had taken every ounce of energy Mike possessed to stop Lamont from running after her. With Lamont's temper, everyone knew it would have led to the police being called.

"Sissy can handle herself, man. Tomorrow you sit down and talk to her reasonably. Sissy is a smart girl and she wouldn't do nothing to hurt you all, you know that," Mike said.

"It ain't Sissy that I'm worried about, it's Tupac's cousin I'm worried about, I can't believe she'd even consider going out with somebody like that, the level of disrespect, I still can't get over it,"Lamont said, mostly to himself.

"Well, okay, so he's different from what you had in mind in terms of appearance but remember how different we wanted to be when we were his age,"Mike said.

"Mike, man, you don't get it, it wasn't his appearance so much as his behavior. It left me feeling, I don't know, I guess what I want to say is, he gave me the creeps. I had this feeling in my gut, you know?" Lamont said, sadly. Nobody understood how he felt about his little girl.

After their guests were gone. Evelyn revived the fire in the fireplace and sat down on the long sectional sofa in the family room next to her husband. Lamont laid his head in her lap and she began to stroke his head as she often did when they were in a deep discussion, it helped her to concentrate.

"Honey,"he said softly.

"Yea, baby,"

"Was that guy as bad as he seemed or am I making more out of it than I should,"

"Baby, I'm not sure what just happened, but one thing I do know, I had a bad feeling about him. And feelings don't lie, they're either totally wrong, or totally right, there is no in between. All I know is that when Sissy is around him she gets a little too excited for me and she doesn't listen to us at all. I don't ever recall her just walking outta here like that knowing we didn't approve of what she was doing. Being with him did that, and that is why I don't like him," Evelyn said.

"I would really like to believe that I got the wrong impression about this guy. Judging a person because of the way they look is wrong and..." Evelyn interrupted him,

"No, it wasn't the way he looked, it was his air, his space, it was funked up, he had some kinda funky, scary thing going on. I'm tellin' you. Oooo, I don't know what I'm tellin' ya. I hope to God that I'm wrong about my opinion of him." Lamont stroked her stomach, "baby, do you remember when I first met your parents,"

"Yea, I remember,"Evelyn smiled.

"Well, you know they didn't like me either, remember. In fact, didn't they hate me or something?" he asked teasingly, "and when you got pregnant with Devon, oh my God, I was the devil himself. And baby, remember when your father got mad at me cause I wouldn't cut my hair for the wedding? That was funny. I was suspect until the day we got married. And the next thing I know they were calling me son," Lamont laughed, "but I liked it, they're nice people though. The older I get I understand your father more and more, in fact, I've almost turned into your father." He finished. "Do you remember how intense our love was at that time? Gurl, you had me going, I had a love jones, gurl." he laid her down on the sofa and kissed her passionately. He sucked on her neck, leaving a love bite behind. Just as he began to pull her skirt up over her thighs,

"You two a little old for that ain't 'cha?" Devon scared the hell out of them. Returning from his friends house, they hadn't heard him come in. Evelyn quickly pulled her skirt down as Lamont got up, scrambling to hide the affect their little petting session had on him.

"Boy, what are you doing here, where'd you come from,"

"Uh, huh, almost caught'cha didn't I," he laughed. "You two, I tell ya, I can't leave the house for one minute. Next thing I know you'll be crying on my shoulder where you done gone and gotten yourselves in a family way. Now didn't I just have that talk with you two, I told ya'aw I ain't having that." Devon said shaking his head in pretend disappointment. Lamont distracted him, playfully smacking him upside his head leading to about three minutes of play boxing.

Evelyn loved her some Devon. He was the spitting image of Lamont. This year he entered his second year at Kent State as a pre-law student. He chose to commute, not wanting to eat campus food and loving, as he put it, the provision for girlfriends in two cities.

"Ole man, ole man," he teased his father.

"What,"

"You said, my brotha, and I quote, that as soon as I forked up the three thousand dollars you'd match it so I could get some new wheels. I know I won't be getting a brand new car, but I need something a little more reliable,"Devon said. He didn't know it but she and Lamont decided secretly that the car would be new.

"So, you managed to save up three grand, huh,"Lamont said proudly.

"Now, Dad would I be asking you if I hadn't. You gotta learn that this brotha don't play, trust me, man. When I say I'm gonna do something, I do it,"

"Alright, we go lookin' Friday after work, how's that?" Lamont asked. Devon didn't have any classes on Friday. He worked at Office Max part-time until four thirty on Friday afternoon.

"Can't you guys go on Thursday. The dealers are opened late that night, you'd have more time," Evelyn suggested

"Right, Ma." Devon turned to his father, "I get outta class at three thirty on Thursday, I could be here by four fifteen at the latest. We could be down on the auto mile by four thirty or so, okay Dad,"

"That'll work."

"Aw'height, I'm outta here. I'm going down to Jam Central in the flats. That's exactly what I'll be doing tonight, jammin'," he turned around in a circle showing off his dance moves, "I'm on my way outta here people, I gots ta' get down there before all the nice young ladies are taken, of course nothing happens 'til I get there, you know they all waitin' on me." He was so funny.

"Sweety, see if you see your sister down there, I think I remember hearing her say something to Denise about stopping down there tonight. I wasn't too keen on that boy she went out with, peep her out fo' me bro'," Evelyn said.

"Now when have you two ever been happy about anyone Sissy went out with,"

"Look, just do it, boy." she threw a napkin at him. He ducked, pimp-walked up to her and kissed her on the cheek. His go-tee brushed the side of her mouth. She grabbed his neck and held it there in a playful manner, as she whispered,

"I love you, baby,"

"Now don't get jealous ole man, when you got it, you got it,"

"Get outta here boy, I'm trying to spend some quality time with my wife and you all in the way," Lamont laughed.

"Yeah, now you two listen to me carefully. We don't need no mo' crumb snatchers up in here, remember that will ya, for all our sakes. I gotta keep my inheritance in tac. Somebody gotta have a level head around here 'cause you two certainly don't. A dawg gotta do, what a dawg gotta do." He grabbed an apple off the dining room table as he headed for the back door. They heard Lamont's BMW being cranked up and Lamont shook his head affectionately,

"I didn't tell that knucklehead he could drive my car,"

"Let's not talk about Devon anymore, I got plans for you, baby." she said seductively, a twinkle in her eye that only Lamont could put there.

Chapter Three

"Sup, man. Whaz happenin'" Devon yelled, waving to his friend Sam and his lady, Wanda, as they walked towards the club.

"Sup, partna, What'chew been up to, dawg?" Sam greeted him walking with his arm possessively around his lady. Bad skin and crooked teeth made her about as desirable to him as somebody's grandma, but Sam always thought somebody wanted his broke down looking chick, standing ready to check you if you looked too long.

"Ain't nothing to it, man. Just tryin' to git the party started. Hey Wanda." He said barely glancing at her. He finished carefully locking up his father's ride.

The ole man would have a fit if something happened to his ride. Devon chuckled to himself.

"Look partna let's hook up, have a drink or something before you split, cool," Sam said.

"It's a done deal, bro, holla." As long as Sam was joined at the hip to Wanda like that he had not intentions of stopping by their table, he didn't need no drama in his life tonight.

The night was clear and the breeze from the lake felt refreshing to his skin. He stood there briefly, mesmerized by the movement of the dark liquid called the Cuyahoga River. It rocked purposefully, searching for a destination to empty into, finding one in the great, black abyss, Lake Erie. He thought it strange how differently it appeared at night. What seemed a friendly body of water, waiting for swimmers and boaters in search of summer fun during the day, at night, appeared as a great serpent beast lying in wait to devour whomever happened along its' path. Many reports of drowning while drunk detoured him from consuming more than one drink.

Inside the club Ludicrous rolled lyrics off his tongue as smooth as a vanilla shake. Devon strolled towards the entranceway, conjuring up his sexiest walk. Thoughtfully crafted at home in front of his bedroom mirror, his walk took careful choreography and a lot of practice.

Cliques of young-ladies stood huddled together here and there, in an unassuming manner, positioning themselves so they got first chance with the men coming into the club. He noticed one young-lady standing to the side of the entrance, not one of the usual she was apparently waiting for someone.

"She is fine, go head and ask her her name," he thought, but decided against it. Her smooth, brown skin accentuated by honey blonde hair, was cut short and sexy. He found the color intriguing, not cheap or tacky looking, but added just the right hue to her skin. Unusually long lashes covered big brown eyes. He slowed down just a little as he passed her. He didn't want to but he felt drawn to her.

Walking through the entrance to the club, strangely he hoped she wasn't leaving.

A big burly security guard met him at the door, checking ID's. Another brotha stood next to him collecting the ten dollar cover charge. Devon showed his driver's license, handed over the ten dollars, received a stamp on the back of his hand and walked through to the bar. Still thinking about the girl outside he ordered a drink and settled down on the bar stool.

"What can I get you my man," the bartender asked.

"A white wine spritzer, thanks,"Devon said.

"I'm on it," he said, expertly flipping the wine glass upright.

Two guys sat perched on the stools to his right. They paid the bartender for their drinks and continued their conversation,

"Man she trippin'. She constantly complaining that we never do nothin' togetha, I ain't on dat shadow shit. She 'bout ta run me away, dawg, always whining 'bout us not spending enough time togetha , I don't know what she wants from me. I work twelve hours a day just to keep my business from going under, and I ain't got a lotta time to put into a relationship. What little time I do have left, the Browns got dat," the first brotha said, stirring his drink with his straw.

"I'm feelin' you on that, dawg. If it ain't a booty call I ain't interested. Women are too complicated, dawg," the other said after taking a big gulp from his beer.

"She can never remember the times I do spend wit her. I'm salty, man. Didn't I let her go to the game wit us last Sunday, member dat,"

"Yea, I was pist dat you even bought her and didn't ask. I ain't never took no woman of mine to a game, never will. I can't enjoy myself wit'em there. They always on that romantic shit.. Dat is whimpy, I can't git wit dat." His friend finished. Neither of them was much to look at and they seemed lost and abandoned.

Two young ladies who looked to be in their late twenties sat to the left of him. One had hair piled on top of her head that must have extended itself a foot high. The big ponytail, a hideous pink color which she slung around as she talked, suggesting she thought it looked good. She could have really been quite attractive except for the 'do'. Her friend, tall and average looking with a head full of braids which needed freshening. He thought he noticed a piece of lint in her nape area, stuck in the field of nappy beads that lined the back of her kitchen. He listened for a minute,

"So he tells me that he's only using her for sex. Can you believe that? I think he thought I was suppose to be happy or something, thank him for sexing up another woman cause she good at it. Me, I'm good at holding it all together, so that's why he keeps me around. Dat is rank, gurl. Brothas ain't worth nothin'. Why didn't he tell me all of dis befo' I got dem babies. I already had my lawyer guarnishee his wages, he gon' be salty when he find dat out. I still miss'im tho, I know I sound stupid, don't I,"

"No." Her friend softly replied.

The bartender sat Devon's drink down in front of him, he laid the cash down and left to cruise.

Moving about the club he concentrated on the 'hook-up'. Just as he was about to turn and move to another area of the club, he spotted 'her'. Sitting alone in a booth with a glass of wine on the table in front of her, without thinking, he began walking in her direction,

"What the hell am I going to say to her once I get over there," he thought. With every step he took he became more and more unsure of what he would say. Standing about six feet away he desperately tried to appear casual, that it was merely a coincidence that he stood only inches away. He studied her on the sly. Devon loved women. He loved the way they looked, the softness of their skin, their smooth, childlike voices, the way their hips moved sensually to music.

He wanted a woman as beautiful and as smart as his mother. With her small, perfect size eight frame, she, a one woman giant of a force that held it all together for their family. Without her there no light shone in their home or their lives. His little sister Sissy, even though a pest, was his heart. Being very protective of her he allowed none of his friends around her, except Jimmy, his best friend.

Another girl approached "her" table and sat down for a minute. He watched as they began talking, then, both got up and disappeared into the crowd. The dance floor was packed, scrobe lights flickered across the faces of dancers and he looked to see if anybody he knew was out there.

"Sup, dawg. How long you been here," he felt a hard slap on his back, spilling his drink. Turning around he found his best friend Jimmy standing there with a wide grin on his face.

"Playa, let a playa know when you gonna sneak up on'em like that, dawg," giving Jimmy the handshake they'd invented in high school. "What'chew doin' home, dawg?"

"I needed my transcripts for an internship I'm doing this summer and I knew my mom would be forever mailing them. So, my partna gave me a a ride and, here I am. I called your house and your mom told me you were here."

Jimmy, a light honey colored brotha, medium height with broad shoulders, wavy black hair and a tiny diamond earring in his left ear, considered fine by most if not all women, had this unassuming manner about himself as if he weren't aware of his good looks. They'd known each other since fifth grade when Jimmy's family moved into the old neighborhood. When his parents broke up two years later, Jimmy began spending most of his time at his house and Lamont became a sort of surrogate father to him. They couldn't have been closer if they were brothers.

Jimmy attended Howard University as a pre-law student also, and Devon missed him terribly. Still Jimmy, right now, the way Devon saw it put a halt on his program. Jimmy would have to make himself scarce until such time as Devon could get a dance and the 911.

"You see that," Devon nodded in the direction of the table where she'd sat, the seat remained empty,

"Never mind, dawg, how long you here for?" Devon asked.

"Just for the weekend, bro. I need to turn in the transcript on Monday,"

"Listen, Racheal, you remember Racheal Callahan from school, right? Well, she's giving a party tomorrow night. You on it?"

"Hell yeah, I remember Racheal. Forget the party, I wouldn't mind just seeing her, with that tight ass of hers. On it." Jimmy got pushed into him.

"Excuse me." Her voice was girlish, soft as a cloud and warm as a crackling fire. Frozen still, he managed to nod his head in reply to her apology, watching her every move as she sat down at the table. Occasionally she returned his gaze with a smile.

"She's hot, playa, I'll holla at'chew latta." Jimmy left in search of his own "hook-up".

Devon decided to make his move. Approaching the table apprehensively, he ran some lines through his mind that he might say to her. Truthful and direct he felt the best approach when you really wanted someone,

"Hey, sup," even he could hear the nervousness in his voice.

"Haay," she gave him her prettiest smile. He nodded at her friend sitting across from her in the booth. The friend, a little on the heavy side, with a beautiful face, big, thick, juicy lips had just the right shade of lipstick, she too did a quick critique of him as well.

"This is Brenda and my name is, Chanel. Care to tell us your name," her eyes teased. He went blank for a second, having a hard time processing what she said,

"Devon," he replied weakly. "Can I get you ladies anything from the bar or are you drinking," he noticed that their wine glasses had been removed and in their place lay two small purses, a pack of sour patch kids, an address book and a pencil.

"Not right now, we just finished our drinks. But you're welcome to sit with us if you want." She motioned to the empty section of the booth next to her. Brenda, jumped up suddenly.

"There she is, 'bout time she got here," she said, "Excuse me, ya'aw, let me go and get her, she'll never find us." She headed across the crowded room to a young-lady which strongly resembled Chanel.

"Who's that? You all resemble each other." he observed.

"Oh, that's my sister April." she informed him.

The two girls returned to the table and Chanel introduced Devon to April. Taller and thinner and not nearly as sexy, but cool, he liked her.

"Chanel, you comin' back to my place tonight or you goin' to Mama's," April asked.

"I'll go with you if you let me sleep in the bed, company comes first,"Chanel said.

"Says who? Okay, whatever. Right now I'm getting ready to party, let me get my drink on, we'll be back. Come on, Brenda." The two of them left the table. They were left alone. They sat a few minutes, quietly, each comfortable sitting there without saying a word, listening to music that strangely described one's feelings on a first encounter. Their knees touched under the table and neither bothered to move or apologize.

"Are you the oldest, or is April the oldest," reluctantly breaking the silence between them.

"She is. Most people think I am. I love her, but she's kinda wild, not loose, but wild in a crazy kinda way. I haven't decided whether I like her that way yet 'cause most of the time I'm having too much fun. I keep her from getting into too much trouble. She doesn't seem to know when to quit. Now and then, I have to check her." She spoke lovingly of her sister.

R. Kelly's "Love Slide" enticed everybody onto the dance floor. He tugged at Chanel's hand and she instantly got up and headed for the dance floor. He purposely positioned her in front so that when he turned a certain way he could get a good look at what she was workin' wit. When she moved her hips the way she did, his mouth went dry. She winked at him when she turned and he loved it. He liked being teased by a classy lady such as herself.

A slow jam begin to spin and he pulled her to him. She easliy fit into the curve of his body, as she rested her head on his chest, timidly placing her arms under his. As he looked closely into her face he saw something there he'd never seen in any woman's eyes before, a potential friend. Pulling her closer, pressing her breast deeper into his chest, he placed both arms around her tiny little waist and drowned himself in her scent.

A few minutes later, still holding her, moving just enough so as not to linger in one spot, through a haze of infatuation or maybe even the beginnings of love, he didn't know which, he noticed a crowd gathering at the far end of the club. He turned in the opposite direction, not wanting anything to spoil the moment.

The disruption persisted and he looked over in the direction where the noise came from. Looking up for a brief second he thought he caught a glimpse of his sister, Sissy. It didn't register.

"See if you see your sister down there." He remembered his mom saying earlier.

Reluctantly, he focused on the people headed in that direction forming a crowd he couldn't easily see though. In the center of all the chaos, he could see, stood his sister, Sissy.

"What da hell!" He thought out loud. He disentangled himself from Chanel and made a beeline to the other side of the room. More of the crowd gathered to watch. In his haste to reach Sissy he knocked over a couple of tables, spilling drinks, never looking back. Some people remained at their tables, unable to make their way through the thick crowd. Chanel followed him, though from a distance, unsure what she was running to.

It took him maybe ten seconds to reach Sissy and by then he understood the situation. Some cat was threatening her, possibly the date his mother mentioned.

"Don't come at me wit dat shit. You calling me a lie when I say you was trying to git on dat, bitch! You think I believe dat shit, you ain't seen him since elementary school, den why he all up on you like dat?" This cat grabbed Sissy roughly and smacked her so hard she fell down.

"Brandon, please, don't." She pleaded with him, falling backwards onto the floor. The crowd parted like the red sea, making sure they didn't get in the way of her fall. Instantly, swelling appeared on her face where he smacked her.

"Leave her alone, man. Go home and cool off. Don't disrespect the sustah like that." A young brotha said, as he helped Sissy up and back onto her feet. Brandon was unmoved.

The bum with the rag on his head walked over to Sissy and drew his hand back to punch her again or to frighten her, Devon didn't know which. He did know he was dealing with an animal. He reached over the two heads in front of him, grabbing the bum by his lapel, and jerked him away from Sissy. Devon almost lost his balance but managed to regain it, drawing back to bust this cat square between the eyes. Someone grabbed his arm just as he was coming down on him. He turned around to see Sissy standing there holding his arm.

"Devon, please for me, don't do it, it ain't worth it. I just want to go home." she begged, a pool of unfallen tears swam around inside her eyes, so full they were one would think the eyeball would drown in all those unfallen tears. He searched her face for understanding, but got none. By then Jimmy appeared after pushing his way through the crowd,

"We can take him, dawg," Jimmy shouted

"Ah, it's on now," Sam came running up to them, with Wanda, the broke down, looking chick right on his heels.

"I'll handle dis, bro.. 'preciate dat. I think we straight. I can check'em without fistin'im out like he did my sister." Not wanting the situation to turn into the circus he and his friends were accustomed to when they were violently confronted. He didn't want the police called like the last time. Thoughts quickly revolved around in his head as he contemplated the best solution for this dead wrong situation.

He turned to Sissy and very slowly, but with authority said,

"Sissy.. listen to me carefully, turn around and go get into the car..now Sissy. I have Daddy's car. Go, right now, Sissy fo' all of us get into a lotta trouble, Sissy, go, now!" He commanded, then,

"Jimmy take her outta here," Sissy turned reluctantly.

"On it." Jimmy took her arm and guided her out as she looked over her shoulders with pleading eyes.

Devon turned his attention to the cat with the rag tied around his head. The cat stepped back waiting for the confrontation he knew would come. Devon's clothes were mussed from the near altercation. He straightened himself out. The crowd began to disperse. Some lingered out of curiosity. Brandon stood defiant, hard, threatening and silent, his expression unapologetic.

In a controlled, low pitched voice Devon slowly issued his edict,

"Now, you listen well, my brotha, cause if I have to repeat myself, it won't be with words. From now on, you have nothing to say to my sister, ever!" His fingers only inches away from Brandon's face, "Don't come near her again. Anywhere you think she might be, don't go there. Don't ride by our house, don't walk on my sidewalk. Stay far away cause I know how to stop you, big man. Big man gotta hit women, cause he can't handle men. You sorry, man." Spit came out of his mouth and landed on Brandon's shirt. He pretended not to notice. Devon backed away slowly, turned and walked out of the club. The crowd spread a narrow line for his departure. The burly security guard returned from his cigarette break too late to be of assistance.

On his way to the car Chanel caught up to him. He couldn't think about her right now, as much as he wanted to. Neither said a word. They walked together for a moment in silence. She took his hand, placed a piece of paper in his palm, then closed it and walked away.

Outside, he studied Sissy closely as he approached her and Jimmy leaning against the car. Just as a child grows in your absence and changes, Sissy seemed a stranger to him. The girl he knew would never be caught up in this kind of situation. He hadn't hugged her in a long time, so he made it gentle. Releasing her, he pushed her hair away from her face, blown there by a gentle breeze from the lake. Clinging to him tightly, her racking sobs, shocked him, making him feel even worse.

"Shhh,shhh,shhh, he whispered.

"I can't look at you. I know you're disappointed,"she whimpered. He wasn't sure disappointment could correctly coin the phrase he wanted to use, for the moment he was speechless.

"Sissy," he said finally, "what are you doing hanging out with somebody like that? What are you doing with this guy,"

"He's not always like that, Devon,"

"Sissy, he disrespected you, hell he out right hit you so hard he knocked you down. That wasn't a game of tag in there, Sissy,"

"I'm not stupid, Devon,"

"Sissy, is this the first time he did this to you?" He asked perspiration forming on his forehead. His eye began twitching uncontrollably. Jimmy stood beside them waiting for her answer. Somewhere in the distance he heard the fog horn from a boat slowly making its' way up the Cuyahoga. The river was calm where the Nautica Queen docked, waiting for her next departure. Couples strolled by holding hands enjoying the beautiful scenery.

"Sissy, answer me,"They waited for her answer, neither blinking, for fear they'd miss the answer. The answer came in the form of tears as they made their rapid descent down her cheeks.

"You don't understand, he's not like that all the time," he and Jimmy threw up their hands in disgust.

"Ta hell you say, girl," he hissed, "not like that all the time? One time is too many, Sissy, what the hell is wrong wit you?" He massaged his forehead in an attempt to rub some intelligent, effectual words into his brain, "So, then, this has happened before?" She shook her head, "yes."

"I want you to tell me every sordid detail and you betta tell me the truth."Devon threatened.

He could hear in the distance the sound of stomping feet inside the club as people danced. If it weren't for Sissy he would probably be inside enjoying himself with Chanel. Instead, he was there trying to sort out a mess bigger than he'd ever been faced with.

Chapter Four

Evelyn was dreaming she was back at Tuskegee and was late for or missed an important exam. She pleaded for mercy to a faceless professor. Tossing and turning in bed in an effort to get her point across, her sleep had been fretful.

The ringing telephone, she at first thought to be a school bell, reluctantly leaving her dream world, she realized, her phone was ringing. Last night she forgot to unplug her phone after she heard the kids come in. Strangely, they arrived together, that almost never happened.

On the seventh ring she picked up. At exactly the same time, Sissy picked up the phone extension in her bedroom. Evelyn listened for a moment in the event the call might be for her or Lamont, who lay peacefully beside her.

"Yea, sup," Sissy answered, her voice thick with sleep. She wasn't fully awake, just going through the motions.

"You tell me, baby," the deep voice answered. Evelyn connected the voice to Brandon, remembering the way he walked, talked and breathed, none of which she liked.

"Brandon," Sissy suddenly began to whisper.

"Nobody else betta be callin' you, gurl, cause we got it like dat, don't we, baby," it was more of a demand than a question.

"You know what my brother told you last night, don't chew. When my brother speaks, in this house, everybody listens. You blew it, I cannot understand what makes you go off like that, why you trip like that, it's unreal and so very unnecessary. You knew I was down fo'real," Evelyn strained to hear and understand the conversation.

"Well if ya ask me, I ain't understandin' wha'cho brotha got ta do wit my luv life anyway, you understand what I'm sayin'. If he stay da hell outta my business, I'll stay da hell outta his. I shoulda popped dat nigga when I had da chance,"

"Are you crazy, don't even play like that when you talkin' about my brother, man, sometimes I don't like you at all, you be scarin' me,"she said fearfully. He laughed,

"You know I'm jus' kiddin' wit'chew, baby. I wanna see you, I gotta see you, it's jus like dat, baby," he said tenderly, the sexual innuendo popped out at Evelyn and smacked her right in the center of her forhead.

"You just don't get it do you? You blew it. I gotta hang up fo somebody hear me talkin' to you, I'll call you later," she ended impatiently.

"Yea, cause if I don't hear from you, you will hear from me, baby, peace out." He warned. They both hung up the phone.

Evelyn's mind began to race as she eased the phone down into the cradle, where it rested next to her bed on the night stand. The room, a peaceful color of beige did nothing to calm her. Carefully, moving the covers back so as not to awaken Lamont, she quietly placed her feet on the oriental rug, and in her bare feet she slipped over to the chase lounge that sat in front of the window to retrieve her robe. She could hear activity on the street from her window. Already people were out and about. Next door, already Mrs. Campbell returned from the grocery store and began unloading her groceries. She yelled for her son Kevin to come out and help. The base from a teenager's car stereo bumped loudly as they slowly moved down the street, hoping to see a familiar face. She knew her white neighbors wouldn't appreciate the disturbance.

Evelyn reached the door and eased the lock over, the click she thought would surely awaken Lamont. She turned around slowly, half expecting him to ask her back to bed. His torso moved up and down evenly with every breath that he took as he lay on his back in a deep sleep. Seeing him laying there in the partially lit room, looking sexy as hell, made her want to return to bed. Instead, she silently turned the glass doorknob pulling the door open.

In the hallway she quietly closed the door and headed for Devon's room. Inside his room, she heard Devon's light snoring with the half whistle at the end, as the morning's ray of sunlight beamed across his still body. She hurriedly crossed the room and carefully nudged him,

"Devon, Devon," she whispered, looking over her shoulder, half expecting to see Sissy standing in the doorway. The house was totally quiet except for her own movements. Devon's digital alarm clock read, nine forty-five. It was time for her to get her day started anyway. She shook him again. One of his eyes seemed crusted together, she suspected pink-eye. She would need to reapply his ointment.

"Ma, what you want. This is my only day to sleep in, he complained hoarsely, pulling the covers up over his shoulders. Evelyn sat down on his queen size bed and leaned into him. She hesitated a moment as thoughts scampered directionless through her mind ,like mice with no crack or crevice in which to hide, still they run to and fro, looking anyway.

I shouda popped dat nigga when I had the chance. Evelyn remembered him saying.

"What happened last night," she whispered.

"Why you askin' me 'bout last night, Ma,"

"I overheard a conversation between Sissy and that boy on the phone a few minutes ago. He said something about you not wanting him to talk to Sissy, ever. What's going on, Devon. Please, honey don't lie to me. Something's going on isn't it, I mean with Sissy and that boy," she asked, "Devon, is there something I need to know about Sissy," fear washed over her as she searched Devon's eye, waiting for his answer.

He swung his legs over the side of the bed and reached for his robe. Fastening his robe, his eyes never leaving hers, as he exhaled loudly and plopped heavily onto a chaise lounge Evelyn found at a garage sale. He hesitated as he carefully examined every word he would say to her. Her life seemed to be hanging in the balance as she waited for him to speak. Finally,

"Ma, last night Sissy got knocked around by that guy Brandon at the club," he sighed, relieved to share the information with somebody.

"Knocked around? What do you mean knocked around, as in hit, knocked around," she asked incredulously. Lowering her voice even more, she leaned over,

"Where did he hit Sissy,"

"In the club,"Devon answered.

"No, no," she waved her hands, "I mean, where did he hit her exactly..in the head, on the butt, where," she felt sick.

"He smacked her in the face and knocked her down, Ma. I didn't get to see the whole thing, I caught the tale end."

Evelyn shook her head from side to side in disbelief, not wanting to hear anymore. She inattentively studied the stenciled sailboat pattern and the scene from Lake Erie she'd painted on Devon's walls, while thinking to herself,

"He actually hit my daughter's beautiful face. The face I've kissed a thousand times. The face that smiled at her when she bought home good report cards. The face that cried when she failed her first spelling test in grade school. The face that nuzzled her Daddy's neck and brought him unspeakable joy. The face that bit Devon and Jimmy because they wouldn't let her hang out with them. That face? He smacked that face, my baby's face. A stranger to us all, somebody we didn't even know took the liberty of physically harming her?

It had to be a mistake. Why would he do that. I'll find his mother and have her keep this scoundrel away from my daughter, or else, what?" Suddenly Evelyn, overwhelmed with fear, didn't know what the hell to do.

"Don't tell your father anything about this. I'm afraid of what he might do, I do not want him to end up in jail, plus his heart, oh Lawd..let me think about this for a minute."

" Ma. I'm not sure if that's the end of him, he seems like the type dats gon be hard to get rid of,"Devon said, reflectively.

"I don't know right now, sweety. I just don't know. But for right now we're just going to keep this to ourselves. If you find out anything more, you tell mommy." Devon shook his head in agreement.

Later that morning, preparing pancakes for her family she moved as if in a trance. She could not comprehend what had happened. But one thing she did know, it had changed her life forever. She poured the pancake mix into the bowl, added the egg and buttermilk without thinking. Once the batter was smooth enough she'd stick the sausage back into the oven in order to serve it hot with the pancakes. It was such a routine she didn't have to concentrate.

Today she couldn't stop thinking about Sissy. What would make her daughter keep company with someone like Brandon, she thought.

Is there something wrong with Sissy? she questioned herself, what was she thinking when this boy hit her in the face, was she scared of him, had he threatened her in some way, maybe even raped her, no. She couldn't bare thinking of him touching her daughter in such an intimate way, then, turning around and beating her with the very same hand he'd earlier caressed her with.

What about his family. Maybe they hold some of the answers I need. Do I really know my daughter like I thought I did? Well, he certainly better not get caught coming around here again. Will he really stay away simply because he was told to. This could get complicated. She groaned to herself.

Lamont came into the kitchen, dragging his feet, tired from their long night of partying and love making. He put his arms around her waist and nuzzled her neck. She could smell the toothpaste on his breath from a fresh brushing.

"Did you get the paper off the porch, baby," he asked lazily. His breathing seemed a little labored. Perhaps he'd come down the stairs too quickly. She constantly worried about him,

"You feelin' okay today, baby," she asked.

"Yea, I was just a little lonely when I woke up and you were gone,"he said.

"Sleepy head, you can afford to sleep all day but I gotta fry up some grub for my man," she laughed half heartedly.

"It ain't food I want. You always trying to feed me, gurl,"he said.

"Well I have things to do. I have a little cleaning to do and I might wash a couple loads of clothes. Then we can either go out or stay in, the choice is yours, love." She tried to concentrate on the pancakes as he ran his hand inside her bath robe pressing into her from behind. She turned around, opened her robe, pulled him by his hips and moved the big bulge between his legs across her stomach.

"Come back to bed with me, baby." He softly pleaded. She turned and flipped the pancakes. She turned back and kissed him softly allowing her tongue the pleasure of answering, yes. They heard Sissy on the stairs and quickly parted. If she wasn't careful, Lamont would keep her in bed all day, catching little naps in between his orgasms. He considered it the perfect way to spend a cold, wintry afternoon.

When Sissy mindfully walked into the room Evelyn saw it, immediately. A little swelling on her lower left jaw. To some, barely visible to the eye, but a mother would notice it, especially given the information she had. Sissy also had a slight limp which she disguised by wearing stilleto boots. Her eyes darted over to Lamont to see if he noticed, but by then he was immersed in his newspaper, searching for news about his beloved Browns football team. If Evelyn hadn't been on vacation she wouldn't have had a clue about any of this. She would've happily gone off to work in an existential cloud of delusive security. What if this boy had the power to persuade Sissy to see him again? Her mind was blown just thinking it. With great distress, she realized that if Sissy made the wrong move, all of their lives could be jeopardized.

"Evelyn, Evelyn, Evelyn," Lamont yelled from across the room. Startled, she jumped. She hated it when he yelled that way. After all these years he had to know it scared her shitless. Her voice, lost in her daydream or more appropriately, her nightmare, stuck heavily in her throat like a thick cleaning rag soaked in hazardous cleaning agents, the fumes suffocating her.

"Where's the checkbook, I might as well take care of these bills. What are you thinking about, baby," Lamont asked, somewhat curious.

"Nothing, sweety, nothing. I think I might still be sleepy, and I can't figure out why, I slept well." She lied.

Their night, filled with Barry White, more wine and lovemaking, usually left her feeling exhilarated, but well rested. But, lately, when they made love an overwhelming feeling of fear crept into her room. It's presence hindered her from getting buck wild in bed as she'd always enjoyed doing with her husband. The problem, she worried about his heart condition, often seeing images of herself becoming front page news, "Man Dies In The Arms of His Wife as They Make Love". She knew if that happened to her, unlike Rose on the Golden Girls, one of her favorite shows, she would never make love again. So, her sex life, now somewhat subdued and unfamiliar to them, had to be, because living without her man was not an option.

"Your pancake is ready," she informed him, handing him his plate. He looked at the pancake with appreciation. Sissy took hers and sat across from her father whose head still hung buried in the newspaper.

"Where's your brother, is he coming down now,"Evelyn asked Sissy.

"Uh, huh." Sissy answered, swallowing her food down, half chewing it, using the orange juice to wash down her food , in a hurry to get out of Evelyn's eyesight.

Evelyn looked out of the kitchen window, expressionless. The sun shone brightly through the white snow, which hugged the branches of naked poplar trees. Reaching towards the heavens the trees seemed always closer to God than humans. In the midst of all the sunshine, made brighter as it reflected off the pristine snow covered earth, Evelyn felt rather displaced , like the branches of the trees reaching towards heaven, always dying before.

Any other Saturday morning she would be enjoying breakfast with her family, laughing, talking, and lingering lazily over a cup of coffee as she and her husband anticipated a mid-morning romp in bed. Instead, a dark cloud descended upon her house, like an unexpected thunderstorm on a beautiful summers' day picnic, sending everybody running for cover.

The doorbell rang and Sissy bolted for the door. Over her shoulder she shouted,

"It's Denise, Ma, could you put her a pancake on, too?" Evelyn dropped another pancake on the griddle.

"Haay now, whazup, girl," she greeted Denise.

Haay, it's on, I got my letter," Denise screamed, jumping up and down. Denise, Sissy's best friend, was so tall and lanky she looked like a giraffe galloping clumsily into the kitchen. With her high cheek bones and beautiful eyes Denise should have considered modeling as a career choice.

"No, girl, you didn't," Sissy squealed, "so you going ta Spelman, huh." They began to walk towards the kitchen. "Com'on let's eat'n'talk, Ma fixed some pancakes for you," Sissy reported.

"Ummm, yummy, just what I need, I'm starvin'." Denise rubbed her belly.

"Hey Denise, we just heard you telling Sissy the good news, girl, you all that and a bag of chips," Lamont said, trying to be cool but sounding ridiculous.

"Daddy, stop that, you sound, ridiculous,"Sissy laughed.

"I know you didn't just say I sound stupid after bringing that idiot in here last night. Did she tell you Denise 'bout that Tupac character she's dating, now that's stupid. I notice you didn't come home with that chump last night. My guess is you had to dump his ass, without a doubt that's the smartest thing you've ever done. Don't get mad at me, baby, but a man knows what's going on out there. Listen, tell your brother I said to stop playing so hard with you, you have a little lump there on your jaw. That boy don't know when to stop playing, he plays too much." Nobody said a word. The room was absolutely quiet. Adoring her father the way she did, the truth hurt all the more coming from him. Evelyn realized that she hadn't in fact hidden anything from Lamont, he knew exactly what was going on, he just didn't understand how far wrong it had gone..

"Hey, Denise. Congratulations baby. You always did look like a Spelman woman to me," Evelyn ended the uncomfortable silence. Denise smiled as she ate her pancakes.

"Oh, Ma, you always saying that,"

"Well, it's true. Some people's faces go perfectly with certain HBCU's. I can spot a potential Tuskegee student a mile away, I swear, can't we Lamont?"Evelyn said.

"Yep, and there's one standing right there," he winked at Sissy.

"Sissy, my Mom says that Tuskegee and Spelman aren't that far away from each other," Denise said, as she gulped down her orange juice. Denise looked as if she'd gotten right out of bed and rushed right over. Her sweat suit looked wrinkled and dirty, her hair uncombed, was a nappy mess. Crusted sleep could still be seen in the corners of her eyes. Her personal hygiene would be attended to later in Sissy's room. As best friends they lived at each other's houses, even keeping spare clothes for emergencies.

Devon charged down the steps just as he'd always done since being a boy. Evelyn wondered would he ever realize his age. She could tell by the way he held the phone and talked that he'd met someone new. Darting into the room long enough to give his breakfast order, he swung at his Dad, vying for Lamont's attention.

"Go on,boy." Lamont replied distracted by his newspaper.

"Hey, Dee Dee.What's up wit dat head of yours. You need to git on dat, like yesterday," He swayed away using that sexy stride he'd practiced to perfection.

"Just worry 'bout yo own head. I'm on it." Denise retaliated. She got up to rinse her dishes and placed them in the dishwasher.

"Come on, Devon and get your breakfast." He sat in a corner, isolated, his conversation barely audible, peeked Evelyn's curiosity. Always able to hear regardless of where her children were in the house. She could hear even if they were around the block, God gave all mothers the ability to hear secrets.

"Hey, Chanel let me call you back. Where you headed? Call me back then, let's try to hook up tonight, kay, holla." He picked up his plate and swallowed his food so fast Evelyn was afraid he'd hurt himself.

Sissy began clearing the table. Lamont still engrossed in his paper, sat at the kitchen table but really didn't know what was going on around him. Devon swallowed down the last of his orange juice and rudely belched right into the faces of Sissy and Denise.

"Ooew'wa. Ma make him stop. You are repulsive. Stop it you, you, what are you anyway. Ma. Go away, Devon, you are disgusting," Sissy yelled, hitting him with the dish towel.

"That's da point, or don't you get it. I know you a little slow. Denise help her out, oh I forgot it's the retarded leading the retarded," he winked at them and headed for the stairs.

"You need to quit, Devon." Denise laughed. The phone rang as Devon passed it on his way upstairs.

"Hello, hello..hello." He hung up. Looking at Sissy suspiciously, he motioned for her to come into the foyer.

"Now, I know dat nigga ain't calling here after I told'im not to, right, Sissy," he whispered, looking at the caller identification screen, which read private number.

"How am I supposed to know who it is if they hung up, duuuuhh," she snapped.

"Now, I don't wanna have ta put a whuppin' on him that he'll nev'a forget, but I will if I haf'ta. I'm already having to hold Jimmy and Sam back. They want to kick his ass but I'm thinking that our kick ass days were behind us. I don't wanna see anybody get into any kind of trouble whatsoever, you understand what I'm saying. But now if I need to, I don't need to finish the sentence do I," he said.

"Okay, so I hear you." she replied. He turned towards his mother and said,

"Ma, I'm going over to Jimmy's. Wha'chew cooking for din-din, can I bring Jimmy," he asked.

"Jimmy's home, yes of course bring Jimmy. I'm not sure yet but just bring him." Evelyn said.

"Ma, me and Denise are goin' skatin', okay,"

"It's Denise and I are going skating. Keep your cell phone on in case I need to call. Be careful." She and Sissy needed to talk but this wasn't the time. For the first time ever, she didn't know what to say to her daughter.

Chapter Five

Sissy pushed her way through the crowd as the manager of the skating rink removed the velvet rope form it's hook, that contained the crowd, not allowing them past a certain point. The crowd shoved harder, almost knocking her down, even though they couldn't all walk through the door simultaneously. Still, everybody felt they should walk through first, so they pushed and shoved without reason.

Hating this part of the weekly skating rink visit, it would be great to just walk in, she thought. But the reality of the situation was, they had to wait outside until the previous session's crowd left, making room for the next crowd. In all the confusion of pushing and shoving, she and Denise got separated from each other. Just as well, she thought. During the trip over, they argued about Brandon the entire way over. She needed a break from Denise's condescending attitude.

"Get the hell away from him, Sissy," Denise yelled at her, "why you still thinkin'bout him, talkin'bout him, wantin' ta be wit'im? You too smart fo' dat, Sissy"

"What did I jus' say, Denise. I'm only telling you what happened. I know I can't see him anymore. I know it in my head but my heart is telling me something different. Please, don't turn me off, I need someone to talk to,"Sissy felt like crying.

"What,"Denise tried to soften her tone of voice.

"I don't think it's going to be that easy to break it off. I'm scared,"

"I am too, I heard some things about him." Denise said sympathetically.

Once inside the skating rink she ran over and claimed a vacant bench, she sat down, unzipped her boots, and put her skates on, which she decorated herself. She brought the pair she'd decorated for this girl named Rita. She knew she would come around any minute asking for them.

"Sissy, whaz-up, you got my skates," Rita walked up behind her.

"I'm on it girl, here," she handed her the skates. Rita took a ten from her pocket and gave her the fee she charged for her decorating skills. Good at what she did, she had plenty customers.

"Hey Sissy, whaz-up wit yo' dawg, Brandon," Rita asked.

"Come again," Sissy pretended not to understand.

"Come again my ass. What was up wit dat show he put on at Jam Central last night. That shit was rank. We cool enough to talk about it, right,"

"No, actually we're not,"Sissy glared at her.

"Whateva." Rita walked away with a serious chip on her shoulder.

"The nerve of her to step to me like that. If she was there last night, then that means the whole town was there, by the time she gets finished telling the story. This is so embarrassing." Sissy thought.

Denise skated up beside her,

"Girl, I hate waiting in that line, it's the pits. Somebody pulled my shoe off my heel and it's hurting." Sissy went out to the floor to warm up.

Today Sissy needed to relax and have a little fun. Out on the floor she looked back at Denise and motioned for her to hurry up. The music rocked the house, moving her body into motion. Working her wheels against the wooden floor was fun and she returned every Saturday to put new moves together. Denise joined her. She warmed up her first round and then began her fancy crosses. A cutey skated up beside her and from his facial expression, Sissy knew he wanted to skate as a couple,

"Naw, bro, maybe later. I jus' got here." Denise declined..

"I know you think I'm stupid, don't 'chew," she asked Denise.

"Naw, I don't think you're stupid, I think you make some stupid moves though and some bad choices. I don't think you really understand where this could lead, cause if you did, you'd end it, no matter what." Denise crossed over and around Sissy and began skating backwards. She faced Sissy,

"Look at you, you're beautiful, I mean really beautiful. Why you puttin' yo'self out there like that,"

"If I knew the answer to that then we wouldn't be having this conversation, would we? I don't know

Neicey, I remember how nice he was when we first starting being a couple. Remember the flowers, the gifts and remember how he never let me walk anywhere? Was that all a front, Neicey?"she asked, reflectively.

"That's how dey rope you in, girl, it wasn't real."Denise said, matter of factly.

Growing impatient, the guy returned for Denise to skate with him. She took his hand and away they went. For a while Sissy got caught up in circling the rink, practicing new moves. Feelings of isolation, especially strong, in the midst of a crowd were commonplace since her relationship with Brandon began. A lot of the drama between her and Brandon she dared not discuss with anyone. People might wonder about her mental stability or lack thereof. What had she done to put herself in harms way, most people would think, some even expressing that sentiment. So, she clung to this dark secret, well hidden until now.

"If I see him, nobody can know." she thought, as she skated around and between people who were barely moving on the floor.

A while later Denise caught up with her and they went over to the snack counter, got in the line to order hamburgers and fries.

"He's a cutey," Sissy hunched Denise.

"Yea, we exchanged numbers, girl. I love his eyes, they are so sexy," Denise said dreamily.

"Where does he live," Sissy asked as she thought about the conversation they'd had earlier about Brandon.

"What difference does it make where he lives, I like him. It ain't like Brandon lives in Pepper Pike or something, don't even go there, Sissy," Denise may have laughed, however she couldn't have been more serious. Sissy was always trying to size people up according to where they lived, Denise thought, what is that about?

"Girl, will you get off the subject of Brandon, you wearin' me out wit' dat," Sissy retaliated. It wasn't as though Denise hadn't had a bad relationship or two herself in the past. Still, Sissy had to admit, Denise knew when to get out. That was the difference between the two of them. It seemed easier for Denise to break a bad relationship off when it went sour.

"One hot dog..with fries on the side and a coke...oh yea, and I'll have one of those chocolate chip cookies, please." Sissy said, pointing. She paid for her order and looked around the room for a table.

"Next," the waitress yelled.

"I'm gon' be sittin' right over there," she said to Denise.

"'Kay," Denise replied as she stepped up to place her order. Sissy found a table with two empty seats and put her tray down, when she recognized some kids from her school sitting at a nearby table. Taking the first few bites of her food she heard the whispering and realized they were talking about her.

"No, no, no he pushed her and that's how she fell backwards," one girl said.

"Oh, I heard that she slapped him first and that's why he pushed her down,"another said.

"Both of ya'aw wrong, he punched her in the face and he punched her so hard until she fell backwards, now that's what really happened. Either way he dissed her. You should'a seen it." the third girl finished.

Everybody, glad to see the school's academic star disrespected that way, made it hard for Sissy to hold her head up.

She'd always done well in school and as a result, competed for the top spot as valedictorian of her graduating class. Highly respected by teachers and peers, the change in her status bothered her. Usually the teachers pet, other students were happy to see her go down.

"I think I'm gonna go out wit'im, girl," Denise said, sitting her tray down.

"Wit' who," Sissy asked, happy for the destraction.

"Larry, that's his name, Larry. The guy I was skating wit'. I'm on it," Denise said dreamily.

"He is fine, now. Get on dat, girl. What school does he go to,"

"Collinwood, he's a graduating senior. He needs a prom date too. I think he's gonna ask, if he don't I swear I'll go by myself. I swear, I will not go with somebody I can't stand,"

"Girl, it ain't gonna come to that, it's still early yet. You can start worrying 'bout that later,"

"What about you, you ain't plannin' on still bein' wit him are you," Denise's eyes narrowed as she waited for the answer.

"Well, what if I did go to the prom wit'im, assuming he'd go,"she said guardedly.

"I can't believe you,"Denise threw up her hands in despair.

"I told you it's over,"

"Yea, but do you really mean it." Denise hissed at her, taking another bite from her burger. Within seconds of swallowing the last bit of her burger, he walked through the door.

Chapter Six

It didn't take much convincing on Brandon's part to get Sissy to leave with him. As they sped down Chagrin Boulevard, Sissy agonized over Denise's response to her going with Brandon. The disappointment and disbelief that washed over Denise's face, haunted her. She wondered how she would stop this destructive behavior, she really didn't want to go, it was just easier this way.

"Get over here, gurl," Brandon said, patting the seat beside him. She knew it wasn't right to disregard the feelings of her love one, but she couldn't seem to stop herself.

"How'd you know where I was," she asked.

"Where are you every Saturday at two o'clock in the afternoon," he knew her schedule.

"I'm not suppose to be with you, you know that," she felt his hand caressing her shoulder. It felt good.

"So," he answered, driving aimlessly down the street. He reached over and turned up the CD player in his customized 57 chevy. DeAngelo sang, "How Does It Feel." There it was again, the disdain he felt for anyone or anything which threatened his position of authority. He fought authority figures and their demands with the vigor of a hunted rat who found itself trapped. If authority figures said black, then he'd say white, just for the hell of it. This attitude made it nearly impossible for Brandon to fit in with mainstream anything, whether it be school, teachers, police, anybody. Which explained why at nineteen he still hadn't graduated from high school. If the truth be told Brandon was a misfit, a black James Dean type, if you will. Always playing the character who didn't get along in society and whose ending, always predictably grim. His profound disregard for societal rules Sissy found attractive, even a little dangerous, but sometimes inconvenient.

"You really don't care if I get into trouble do you, as long as you get your way,"

"Damn straight, da las'time I looked, der was only two people in dis' relationship. I can't concern myself wit' all da niggas dat's tryin' ta involve dem'selves in my bi'ness." He responded, a devilish twinkle in his eye. She loved that twinkle and often did things she had no business doing as a result of that very twinkle.

A virgin when they met, her limited knowledge of sex came from her mother's teachings, and, from sneaking out into the hallway, listening to her parents at night, when they thought she was fast asleep. The laborious huffing, puffing and groaning, the tell- tell squeaking of bed springs, persuaded Sissy that sex was something she could wait for marriage to experience, as it seemed to her, a rather awkward, hodge-podge of calisthenics. Still, her mother tried her best to make the act seem desirable, if not practical, explaining her take on sex,

"You see Sissy, God invented sex, so sex is a good thing. However, baby, with pleasure comes responsibility. He designed it around the family unit to protect both partners from pain, disease and deceit. One partner per life time, is the ideal situation and the way God planned it, unless one partner dies prematurely. This arrangement not only protects the partners, but the family unit as well. Once a woman and a man swap fluids during a sexual encounter they are bonded together by that exchange. The intimate exchanging of fluids is what makes partners want each other again and again, sniffing, if you will behind each other because they have been connected and bonded by the exchange of bodily fluids." Her mother's spin on the situation only left Sissy more confused, yet had a ring of truth to it.

Knowing that she had no intention of marrying Brandon, the relationship, felt like a boat adrift, without a destination. He represented a whole other world to her, one she enjoyed dabbling in. But later, she wanted to return to the comfort of her upscale, suburban, home, with its' manicured lawn, faux painted walls, shiny wooden floors, professionally tailored drapes and pricey antique furniture. In most circles her family would be considered, privileged. His world provided the excitement her world lacked, but her world could offer the means and the security of a real future, his world lacked.

Brandon turned his 57 Chevy down a Hundred-Forty Seventh Street in the Mount Pleasant area of

Cleveland, where he lived in a tiny three bedroom bungalow with his mother and younger brother. Riding along in the prized fifty-seven Chevy, Sissy wondered about how Brandon afforded the car, with it's original leather seats and polished chrome. It was Brandon's pride and joy, but something the average person couldn't afford. An antique, valued at fifty thousand dollars in pristine condition, she cringed when she thought of how he might be supporting such a luxury toy. So, the question, where did the money come from, always unanswered, she wrote off as none of her concern. Even if she'd ask, there would be no plausible answer. Brandon had no source of income, at least any he could speak of publicly.

His mother, Constance Jones scraped out a living cleaning offices at night. Barely making enough money to pay rent, put a little food on the table and keep a bottle of scotch tucked away in the back of their roach infested kitchen cabinet. To help make ends meet, Mrs. Jones slept with different men, forcing Brandon's younger brother, Jason to call them, "uncle."

They pulled into the driveway as the next-door neighbor's dog began barking loudly, which he always did whenever he heard a car approaching. Litter lay scattered across the un-kept lawn, a huge hole in the screen door stared persistently from the front of the house, covered in peeling paint. As they let themselves inside, Sissy discreetly felt around inside her purse for her birth control pills and condom she would later beg Brandon to wear. Silently she thanked Denise for not allowing her to be stupid,

"Did you make him wear a condom, Sissy," Denise persisted, when she found out she'd slept with him.

"Stop yellin', I will next time. It all happened so fast until..I know what I'm doin', I'm in love, Denise,"

"I know you not tellin' me you laid down wit'him naked like dat, fuck dat love shit. You tellin' me you didn't make'im wear nuttin'? Gurl, are you crazy! What if you get pregnant, den wha'chew gon' do,

"I'm not gon' get pregnant Neicey..."

"Sissy the world is full of gurls who didn't think it would happen to them. They dumb enough to believe the sperm will just swim against the current just cause they say so. But you right, girlfriend, you not gon' get pregnant cause you goin' to the doctor." Scared to death, the next week she went to Denise's doctor, paid the fifty dollars, got her pills and bought a box of condoms for double measure. The pills Brandon knew nothing about, he actually believed she wanted a baby.

Her delimma, if you could call it that, was her parents forbade her keeping company at the home of any man, especially with no one else present. Being the resourceful little sneak that she was she found ways around that rule.

"Wha'chew thinkin'bout, baby," he asked, popping a CD into the player, removing his shirt, getting prepared to sex her up. After wading her way through the dirty kitchen, with it's mile high pile of dirty dishes and the living room's sagging sofa, stained rug and dirty windows, she again felt relieved she'd made it to Brandon's room without being accosted by any creeping, crawling, critters, although she knew they only waited for darkness to come.

"I'm still mad at you about last night. I don't even know why I'm here, in fact I shouldn't be, after the way you dissed me at that club last night. I'm still salty'bout that. And don't tell me that I'm making more out of it than I should," she said finally, adjusting herself on the sinking mattress. He bent down and kissed her softly the way she liked. That kind of weak apology hadn't worked on her in months and she resented him for resorting to such a pathetic means of correcting a horrendous wrong. She didn't know why she was there, except, when she looked into his eyes she remembered.

The first time Brandon walked by her at the mall, where despite the objections of Evelyn, she and Denise spent a good portion of their Saturday afternoons. Watching him closely, Sissy felt the bolts of electricity strike her in places unknown to her, awakening parts within her which, until that moment, remained dormant.

On a beautiful fall afternoon in Cleveland, from the force of wind, giant oak trees and their rustling leaves displayed their spectacle of colors, brilliant red, oranges, and yellows. The wind, swaying back and forth in the tall maple and ficus trees, made it the perfect back drop for squandering one's day away. They'd been sitting outside the Arab clothing store, the one where you were required to turn in your shopping bags from previous purchases to a total stranger for the privilege of shopping in their store, when he sauntered by. Pimp-walking down the corridor, she noticed he'd taken out time to put a different spin on the walk, dipping his right leg just so, making her particularly weak and vulnerable in a strange sorta way. Immediately locking eyes, seeing only each other, just as Tony and Maria had in West Side Story. Neither said a word. Six-feet tall, with a flawless, chocolate complexion, contrasted by even, amazingly white teeth. When he intentionally circled back the second time, he couldn't help himself,

"Hey wha-dup, shorty," he murmurred sexily. Sitting down, she had to bend her head way back on her shoulders in order to look into his eyes.

"Haay," she replied shyly, throwing in a suggestive smile for a good measure.

"I seen you sitting here befo'. You come out here every Saturday,"

"Almost,"

"You was waitin' on me ta say somethin' to you wasn'chew,"he teased.

"Naw, cause this is the first time I saw you,"

"So, you like what you see shorty,"

"Maybe,"

"Okay, so you need ta think on dat one for a minute, huh," he laughed.

"Maybe, maybe not, that's for you to find out,"

"Can you ditch yo' road dawg ova' der and let's discuss it," Denise sat there unamused, she'd hated him from day one.

"No, I can't. She's my gurl, her name is.."

"I'm only interested in yo' name, not hers. What's your name."

"Serrita, Serrita Hill," her smile bubbled over like bubbles from a freshly uncorked bottle of champagne.

"Serrita... nice. Serrita, can you hook a brotha up with the 911,"

"Nope, but you can give me your number, I'll call you..straight up I will,"

"On it," he scratched the number out on a torn piece of paper from the clothing bag he carried his new purchases in.

"I'll call you," she said, tucking the paper in the pocket of her too tight jeans.

"Kay, I'm puttin' it in da bank." He said, winking as he walked away from her. She knew, just by the way he spoke and held his lips, that he knew how to kiss a girl.

Kissing, so important to her, she only knew of one other person who'd mastered the skill, so good, he became the standard by which all other men were measured, and that was, William Fulton. Billy, as everyone called him, was her first boyfriend and the only man, in her opinion who understood the art of kissing. When Billy came over, in a darkened corner of her basement, they experimented with different styles, until they discovered the Cadillac of all kisses. She thought she loved him. He, so tall, she sat on his lap in order to comfortably reach his mouth and it was in this position, one day, her father stumbled upon them and rudely interrupted the most sensual kiss she'd ever received.

Not wanting to take her virginity, Billy, without explanation, just up and left her. Sitting in the solitude of the darkened, basement alone, wondering what she'd done wrong, she languished in a pool of tears, believing that she would never be kissed like that again, her belief had been correct, she hadn't. And so, as Brandon lowered her body onto the bed, his dark, slender fingers, skillfully caressed the intimate folds and secret crevices of her body, she found herself being lulled into a reverie of arms and legs, strangely intertwined in a knot of love. Oddly, it wasn't Brandon she saw, but Billy.

Chapter Seven

Sissy folded her acceptance letter from Tuskegee University and carefully placed it in the pocket of her notebook, where Brandon would never find it. His irrational behavior, unapologetically escalating, turned for the worse when she unwittingly called Billy's name while they made love. Brandon knew Billy was dead, had been dead now for three years, dying of a heroine overdose. Even her dreams were no longer her own. Now, he followed her everywhere, called her constantly and even stalked her, at least that's what Denise called it.

What should have been a time of jubilant celebration, instead, required being kept on the down low, treated as top secret, making clearance essential before disclosure. Carrying around an illusion of marriage and children, she dare not tell Brandon about her plans for college. If he couldn't ruin her plans, then he'd come to the campus and ruin her life, he'd told her so.

Her parents met at Tuskegee University and so the pride they felt was in knowing that a great tradition was being past down to the next generation. Their daughter not only accepted there, but the promise of the prestigious president's scholarship had been more than they'd ever hoped for.

They'd been waiting for her when she returned home, a week ago, Saturday. So excited, neglecting to ask her why she had been so late getting home, and why she returned home walking, after leaving the house in Denise's car. Her mother stood anxiously in the doorway,

"Guess what, guess what," her mother hollered in that squeaky, adulated voice of hers, the one that annoyed Sissy, because, it reminded her of rubber tennis shoes, squeaking on especially dry surfaces, making her flesh crawl. Still, she wondered what all the commotion could be about. Her father, with the familiar, sneaky grin on his face, the one he always wore at every surprise party, a dead giveaway that something exciting had taken place.

"You got a letter today," her father blurted out. True to his nature, try as he might, he couldn't keep a secret. Her mother nudged him in his side, "Oops, sorry," he apologized.

"He is so cute," Sissy thought to herself. "they both are." She watched them lovingly.

"Mom, Dad, whaz-up, is that an acceptance letter or somethin'," she asked, not having the patience to play their little waiting game, "did I get into...Tuskegee. Is that from Tuskegee,

"Sweety, yes, yes, yes, it is! My baby is going to our Alma Mater and she got herself the presidential scholarship. You bad, girl, you bad," her mother sang, waving the letter in the air. Meanwhile, her father did that stupid little dance he always did at the old folks' parties, called the football.

"I can't believe it, I got the scholarship, are you sure," Sissy said, imagining herself strolling through the quaint, southern campus. Not having read the letter for herself, going strictly on what her parents told her, she reached for the letter and sat down to read it.

The connection she felt towards the college was established the minute she set foot there when her parents took her to visit. The stories, she'd read and heard, the history, Booker T. Washington's house, still standing with dignity across the street from the campus, and George Washington Carver's Museum, all served to distinguish it from any other campus she'd ever seen. The buildings, many built by the hands of former students who'd long gone to their graves. Students passing the burial site which sat in the middle of campus, of Washington and Carver, felt privileged to be part of such a legacy as great as that. Not to mention the mesmerizing, and infamous bronze statue of Washington removing the cape of ignorance from the eyes of a slave. Sissy found the symbolism nothing less than astonishing. While walking around the campus, she just knew she felt their spirits pushing her on, towards the mark of excellence. In fact, she imagined, as she'd heard many Tuskegee students witnessed to, actually feeling their hands on her back, pushing her, saying, "Little Black girl, pick up that baton and run, run on, make us proud."

Now, her parents were telling her she'd been accepted there, receiving a full scholarship no less.

She pressed the letter tightly to her chest, hugging the paper, envisioning keeping the legacy alive.

Devon walked into the room just as her father gathered the family in a circle and Lamont directed them to all hold hands as he said a prayer of thanksgiving, for the good news they'd received.

"Father, God we thank you for this day. For this is a day that you have made, we will rejoice in it and be glad. Forgive us Lord for our neglect in thy service, forgive us for our sinful ways, and give us the spirit of repentance and correction. Teach us thy ways, and help us to abandon our own ways as they are not your ways. We love you, we adore you and we thank you for this miracle in our lives that was only made possible by you, for we know that it was nothing we did to deserve it, thank you Father, we give you all the glory, in the name of Jesus, we pray."

Lamont finished his prayer, and wiped his eye with the back of his hand, as a tear threatened to fall. Sissy knew they would all be made to get up on Sunday morning and attend church service, she thought she liked that idea.

"We're going out to celebrate, baby girl, where do you want to go," Her Father asked, rubbing his hands together in anticipation of a favorite meal.

"Well, I want to go to.." Devon began.

"Nobody asked you, bro, we already celebrated your accomplishments, now it's Sissy's turn," Lamont interrupted him.

"Now, Sissy keep a brotha in mind when you're choosing da spot, remember, I put myself in great jeopardy when I lied for you, you remember the time, when you came in late..oops I wasn't suppose to tell dat was I," Devon laughed, hugging her neck and dragging her across the room where he could whisper his request. She hoped he wouldn't be disappointed,

"Ma, would you mind if we stayed home and had some of your fried catfish, that's what I really want for dinner. Devon, I'll take you out to dinner once I start making all dat money as a doctor, fo'give me, bro,"

"Hey, It's your day, go fo'it.. Besides, I feel you on dat, Ma can really hook a brotha up wit' some catfish, can I bring Jimmy,"

"Of course you can," Evelyn answered, as she pulled Sissy towards the sofa in the family room, craving some cuddling time with her daughter. The two sat down and she hugged her daughter tightly. Sissy settled into her mother's arms and rested her head on Evelyn's chest. As her mother spoke to Devon and her father, Sissy could feel the vibration of her voice against her cheek, she found it comforting.

"Take the catfish out of the freezer, Devon," and to Sissy she said, "Oh, sweety mommy is more excited about your life than you are. One day when you're all grown up with children of your own, you'll find out, mothers are like that, living vicariously through their children. Anybody who says they don't is either lying or isn't involved on any level. I see myself one day, leaving my job to help you out around your office. I want to decorate your office on a very grand scale, like my friend Clyde's office in Cincinnati. I already have it pictured in my mind. On the walls, I want to do a sky blue and vanilla, very calming colors. Of course we'll throw in some bolder accent colors with pillows.

I could be your secretary or your assistant," Evelyn rambled on.

"Whoa, whoa, ma, I haven't even graduated from high school yet," Sissy teased.

"I know baby, but it's so exciting, my little girl, imagine that, Dr. Hill, Dr. Hill, calling Dr. Hill, please pick up extension 440, code blue, Dr. Hill," Evelyn went on dreamily.

"Dad, do something, quick, she's having that dream again. You know the one about an office that doesn't exist, painting and wallpapering a wall that doesn't exist. She's buying furniture and office supplies, come in here quick, Dad.. call her psychiatrist and tell'im to phone her some Valium in or somethin',"Devon laughed.

"Leave her alone and let her dream, I like that dream as a matter of fact." Lamont said. Sissy smiled to herself as she drifted off. Entering a trance like state, she felt her father approach them with a blanket, which he quietly draped over the two of them, and as he did, she felt the power of his love push her deeper into a peaceful abyss. Once again, Billy came to her.

She closed out her thoughts of Billy and her family as the last bell of the day was only minutes away. The classroom, felt empty, due to the majority of students having gone down to the basketball state finals. The school chartered a bus, parents and chaperones were summoned, school spirit, pumped up in anticipation of putting on a good showing for the TV cameras, as the game would be televised. And then, she experienced a startling shift in her thoughts, rolling down the mountainside of her imagination, tumbling, dangerously like unrestrained boulders, sure to kill.

Lately she'd been having visions of killing Brandon. Nothing detailed. Just putting the vision into perspective such as, dreams of how loudly she would scream while standing over his lifeless body, fainting, which would add just the right touch of drama to a sordid ending that was seemingly inevitable.

She felt no guilt for having such thoughts, for he'd forced her to this place. Doing everything she could to please him, he'd exhausted her complete repertoire of submissive behavior. Developing what some coined as, "anxiety attacks," everytime she thought of the abuse she endured, she sweated profusely. The shortness of breath which followed, along with a rapid heartbeat, finally convinced her she needed to let her Mom know. Never having swallowed a pill in her life, it took a lot of practice for her to learn how to get the pill down, before all the water disappeared.

To the few students remaining behind, her teacher, Mrs. Brown spoke,

"Okay, class, we have exactly fifteen minutes to the bell. Make sure your petri dishes are covered and labeled for easy identification on Friday. Homework is on the board, copy it. I don't want anyone coming to me later saying they didn't know they had a homework assignment. Put your hand down Greta, don't worry about the students who aren't here, worry about Greta." said Mrs. Brown, too tired to hide her annoyance.

"Bitch, who she think she talkin' to," Greta mumbled, the residuals coasted, in broken syllables back to Mrs. Brown.

"Excuse me, Greta, did you have something to say, speak up," Mrs. Brown checked her.

"Naw, I ain't say nothin',"the spoiled brat replied. Greta, the daughter of a local politician thought she was all that. Her parents spoiled her until she stunk, badly. Everybody hated her, but tolerated her because her parents had pull. Teachers, found themselves vying to be part of Greta's entourage because of her family's influence, all except Mrs. Brown, who cared nothing about Greta's parents and their "pull." Everybody was the same in Mrs. Brown's classroom.

"Tomorrow in lecture bring your completed assignments with you. I don't want them in your locker, and no, you cannot have time during class to complete your homework, so don't ask." She finished.

Sissy didn't know how it happened but it always did. Landing the position as Mrs. Brown's class pet wasn't an easy task, as she allowed no one to get close to her. Having rules in her classroom that no parent successfully challenged, and expecting everyone to give one-hundred and ten percent of themselves, made her the hated one.

As the top student Sissy often stayed behind to help Mrs. Brown grade papers or whatever she needed doing. Today Mrs. Brown requested that she stay behind to help another student, Justin with the lab assignment he'd missed while out with the flu.

When the bell rang, she and Justin moved to the back of the lab, closer to the storage closet, making it convenient to gather the things they needed to complete the lab assignment. She went to the basket where Mrs. Brown kept her previous lab assignment worksheets.

"Read the list off to me Serrita, I'll get everything." Justin said. Being the cutey pie that he was often aroused feelings of sensuality towards him, that she couldn't help having. A dream of a hunk, with big rippling muscles, he could be labeled a bit conceited, yet everybody liked him. As the star of the football team she was one of many girls who fantasized about Justin. She felt it a privilege to help with the missing assignments.

"I tell ya what, I have two sheets. You take the top half and I'll take the bottom half of the list, it'll be quicker that way," she said trying to suppress her excitement at being near him. He took the sheet from her and mindlessly walked to the storage closet. Sissy took a Bunsen burner, hooked it up to the gas, turned the handle and started the flame. She grabbed the calibrated, glass container and rinsed out the residue from the bottom.

At three forty-five that afternoon, totally immersed in the assignment, writing down the results as they developed, coming to the last page, their work finally drew to an end,

"Thanks, Serrita. When I'm working with you, I actually understand this stuff. Hey, what about a bite to eat when we're done, my treat. I don't have to be at work until five. I can drop you at home afterwards." He said, as they accidentally bumped heads. Both laughed until,

"She already got a ride, dawg," his voice, low and sinister, like that of the devil, chilled the air around them. Leaving behind an icy stench, which instantly formed cicles in the hairs of her nose.

"Hay, baby," she replied weakly. Unable to control the shaking in her voice, she never noticed the puzzled expression on Justin's face.

"Sup, my man," Justin reached for Brandon's hand, but was ignored. He looked at Sissy questioningly, she looked down, unable to meet his confounded gaze. She prayed Brandon wouldn't go off, right there in the chemistry lab, in front of the school's star athlete.

Mrs. Brown suddenly breezed back into the room after taking a quick break from grading papers,

"Kay, guys. You about finished? My husband will be here shortly. Oh, hello, young man, can I help you or are you a friend," Mrs. Brown said. As perceptive as she was, surely she too felt the icy air and its' stench. What came across was, total ignorance to this, a potential powder keg of a moment. Sissy felt positive that it was an act.

"Naw, dis' is my gurl," Brandon nodded in Sissy's direction. Standing there, his doo-rag covered head, arms layered with tattoos, the meaning of which, only a certain element of society would understand and the recent installation of a gold tooth, made it difficult for Mrs. Brown to pair her star student with such a character.

"Mrs. Brown, this is Brandon," Sissy said.

"Okay, how are you, Brandon? Are you a student here," Brandon didn't answer her, he simply nodded, no.

"I'll holla at'cha lata'," he made a sudden exist. She thought of running away.

Chapter Eight

Sissy stuffed her notebook inside her book-bag. Pushing down hard, as hard as she wanted to smack Brandon in his face. Growing weary of his insane display of affection, she knew something was seriously wrong with his way of loving her. Thank God he'd left, but she knew she'd get burned tomorrow.

Closing the lab door behind her, checking to make sure it was locked as she'd been instructed by Mrs. Brown. Outside, the hallway was quiet and deserted, even administrators were at the finals. Turning the corner, she headed towards her locker, needing her English book for tomorrow's assignment,

"Bitch,"a big, black powerful fist which she didn't know at the time belonged to Brandon, came crashing down into her face. The sound of flesh upon flesh, making contact in such a violent way felt foreign to her, but after having heard it she would never forget the sound. So powerful was the blow, she felt herself slipping from consciousness as stars formed inside the darkened area, which appeared whenever she shut her eyes tightly. She put her hand up to her bleeding nose and swollen eye, searching for the familiar parts of her face as if a stranger to them, for her vision had been impaired by the blow. He then grabbed her hair, pulling it he forced her to her knees.

"Brandon? What's wrong, baby," she cried, pitifully.

"Don't hand me dat baby shit, you fuckin'im, ain't'chew,"he stood over her. He pulled her head back, forcing her to look up at him. He loved seeing her in this position, submissive, under his control.

"Brandon, listen to me..how could you say somethin' like that..you know it's you I love? He's just somebody I helped with classwork, my teacher asked me ta help'im," she pleaded.

"Did'cho teacher tell you ta fuck'im too, Sissy? Was dat part of da' assignment, bitch," he hissed. Eyes glazed over with rage, they were cold, empty and void of any feeling. It seemed someone else took over his body. At that moment, she realized that all this time she'd been dealing with a crazy man and she tried to imagine how badly she'd come out of this, if she came out at all.

"Of course not, Brandon, please, my nose is bleedin', baby,"

"I saw you, the two of ya' all chummy, hugged up, his head touching yours. It looked like you been fuckin'im to me, gurl. You ain't nuttin'but a ho, just like my Momma,"he snarled. She thought about Mrs. Jones, with her blonde hair weave, too tight dresses and her whiskey slurred conversation. True, she hadn't been a model of a mother, but certainly she never dreamed this would be the effect she had on her children.

Her gut instinct told her, this was going to be bad and no amount of conversation would distract him. Again, she thought about Billy, his tender kisses, his protective hands and the gentle way he touched her. For a second or two, she felt him there with her. Her delirium left her a measure of sanity, admitting to herself Billy would never be there again in this life.

He took his foot and pressed it hard into her chest, pushing her down, forcing her to lay with her back on the cold, dirty, tiled floor. He pressed her in the chest again, hard, then began a light kicking motion, tapping lightly, at first, progressively it grew harder and harder, taunting her. She grabbed his foot, holding on for dear life. He stumbled, almost falling, balancing himself on the wall.

"Brandon, please, Brandon don't," she pleaded, grappling for a little time, giving herself a chance to think. He got his balance and reached down, snatching her by her Tshirt, pulling her up. At that point she tried to scream, but he quickly covered her mouth with the nasty doo-rag he wore on his head. She could smell the stench of the oil from his scalp, mixed with his sweat and she gagged. She bit down on his hand, and he took his fist and hit her, so hard, fresh new stars formed in front of her eyes, her head wouldn't stop spinning. Now her lip bled as well. He drug her down the hall to the nurses office and opened the door. She thought all office doors were locked after school hours, yet he so casually opened this one as if it had been prearranged. No custodian or anybody seemed to be around. He picked her up and pushed her inside the clinic. She fell onto the clinic chaise lounge, the big green, leather one. She remembered laying on that very lounger when she had been sick with the flu. After the nurse contacted her mom, she'd come to pick Sissy up and together they'd spent the next few days of her recovery in her bedroom. Her mother bought her tea and soup. She hugged her and spoke soothing accolades into her life as she waited by her daughter's beside for the one-hundred and three- degree temperature to break.

Pinning her down on the lounger with his knee, fighting her struggle to escape, he drew back his fist and once again slammed it into her face. Her hands ceased to flail. Still, her body shook from him pulling her back and forth, as he mounted her. Holding both of her hands with his one, he used the other to reach underneath her skirt, roughly pulling her panties down, scratching her legs intermittently.

When she regained partial consciousness, she could feel that her legs were spread open as he pushed his penis violently in and out of her, as if he were trying to kill something. The familiar smell of lovemaking, which once had excited her, now she found repulsive. She kept her eyes closed as he violated her body, throwing her about like an inanimate rag doll, void of human feelings, she thought about dying. It would be an outcome of which, not only was possible but with each passing moment she embraced as a surety.

One thing for sure, she thought, the old adage which says, rape isn't about sex, wasn't true in her case. The bum enjoyed it. Feeling the warm trickle of semen running down her inner thigh, with each twist and turn of the slimy liquid running down her thigh, she felt it cutting her, inside, forming giblet pieces of her heart, lungs and stomach. Suddenly he stopped,

"Baby, baby, I didn't mean fo' it ta go dat far. I didn't. I'm not sure wha' happened. You okay? You gotta stop screwing wit' my head like dat, gurl. You know I'm in luv wit'chew. Dat was da bomb," He mumbled sheepishly. With her vision slowly returning, she felt it a shame that the very first thing she saw, had to be him. As he climbed off from on top of her, disheveled and looking every bit the part of a scuzbucket, cowardly and wimpy, "Your lip is bleedin', don't move." He said as Sissy tried to sit up when she really wanted to lie down and weep throughout eternity.. She knew she had to try and move, or else she would never, ever get up again.

Chapter Nine

An empty promise of love undisturbed by this act of violence against her, had been her only means of escape. It always worked because he needed to hear it just that badly. Telling him that she'd wait for his call the next day relieved him of a good portion of the anxiety he felt, having just raped her only hours before. When she'd looked into the old faded mirror over the clinic's sink, what she saw sent her into a spiral of despair. Her face which she'd always been told was a pretty face, she thought, might possibly be scarred for life. Her eyelids, three times their normal size made her look like a monster. Her lip, fat, bleeding and deformed couldn't form the words that she didn't mean anyway. Dried blood, smeared and splattered all over her bruised body, in her hair, under her nails, on her clothes, and now, she needed to get inside the house and up to her bedroom, without being discovered.

Exiting his car farther down the street, hoping no one would notice, he blocked her from leaving the car until he gave his warning,

"Dis is b'tween you an'me, you feelin' me. I'll be salty if dat smart ass brother of yours try ta step ta me fo' any reason. Don't fo'git', me 'n you," Then he had the nerve to pucker his lips, expecting her to willingly plant a kiss on the lips of a man who'd just raped her.

"I won't forget," she pushed towards the chrome door handle, which he blocked to prevent her leaving, until he decided she could go.

"Cause if da nigga does step ta' me..I got somethin' fo' his ass," the long black, slender hands, he'd once tenderly caressed her with in the past, now seemed reptilian to her as he reached underneath the seats, for his gun. Other than her father's gun, which she'd never actually seen up close, kept in a forgotten draw of their dining room armoire, Sissy never knew anybody who had a gun before now. Slinking away from the dangerous object, she thought about how quickly things could change for everybody she held dear to her and with that thought, she bolted from the car.

"Don't fo'git, me 'n you..shorty." She couldn't bring herself to look at him, as he rolled the car slowly alongside her, it felt as if she were being chased by the devil.

She could hear her mother and Devon chatting inside the house when she reached the steps outside the front door. Thinking it might be easier to slip in from the front door right over to the landing of the stairs, which led to her bedroom, she tried the door. It was opened, but when she turned the knob, the door made a loud clicking noise, bringing Evelyn into the foyer to investigate. Sissy's heart sank,

"Wait a minute, I thought I heard something," her mother said to Devon. "Sissy, is that you, baby? Come in here with us, I can't leave the chicken. Sissy? I made you some spaghetti too, come taste," quickly glancing at Sissy, her mother didn't see the trauma to her face and body.

"I'm not hungry right now, ma,"she replied, weakly, not sure what to do next.

"Call your Dad and tell him to pick up those rolls you like so much, come in here sweety. How was your day,"her mother kept busy.

"I don't..I can call'im from upstairs," she murmurred. She felt tired, and just wanted to rest.

"Git 'dem skinny legs of yours in here 'n help us out. We in here sweatin' tryin' ta prepare a nice meal fo' you 'n you can't even come in here and say hi..go on in der ma, make me proud, exert some parental authority," her brother teased. Sissy smiled, because he was funny.

"Be quiet, Devon..Sissy? What's the matter, you not feelin' well," Evelyn laid down the tongues she used to turn the fried chicken with, turned down the volume on the Oprah show and when she returned to the room, she got a good look at Sissy's face,

"What da.. hell, ooooh, Sissy, what happened to your face? Who did this to you?" She moved slowly, almost cautiously towards her daughter, not believing what she saw, "Devon..come here, Devon. Oh my God, look at her face. Sissy tell me, who did this to you?" Her mother gently pulled her to her bosom, not wanting to further hurt her, and soothed her crying daughter, "Who would hurt you like this, tell me sweety, please"

So far Sissy had gotten away without mentioning his name but she knew it wouldn't be long before they all put the pieces together and mayhem would follow.

Upon hearing his mother's reaction, Devon approached them slowly, not knowing what to expect but his gut instinct told him to expect the worse. He took one look at her face and quickly summed up the situation,

"Awh, hell naw, dis nigga..damn'im," Standing in his stocking feet, he spun around and swiftly headed for the closet to get his shoes.

"Devon, Devon, where are you going? You're not leaving this house, Devon," Evelyn's command sounded more like pleading.

"Awh naw, it's on now. I can't listen to you right now, ma. I'm gonna do what I should'a done the other night. Look at her face, ma..look at it! Damn him," his voice trailed off as he headed for the dining room. Not realizing the reason he headed for the dining room, Evelyn relaxed for a second, then suddenly she remembered,

"He's going in there to get yo' Daddy's gun! Devon..don't you dare. Listen to me, baby..Devon are you listening to me,"he whizzed by them, grabbing his shoes, left sitting by the front door. Sissy saw the cold black thing hanging from his hand, sending chills up her spine. He held it casually as he slipped into his shoes. Turning to Sissy he asked,

"Where does the motha' fucka live, Sissy and don't say you don't know. I can find out," the anger made his voice shake.

"Sissy, don't you tell him nothin'," Evelyn instructed. She'd never seen her mother so frightened before and it frightened her, "Devon, listen to mommy, please. This isn't the way to solve this, violence with violence. I don't want you letting him take your future away from you, that's what he would want, what a lot of people would want. I won't have you throwing away your life this way. Your father and I have worked too hard, please Devon. Let's wait until Daddy get's home, baby and we can all sit down and decide what to do, right now we need to help Sissy,"

"This is what I plan to do, ma, help Sissy. Did you forget, my father has a heart condition. This may just take'im over the top, ma. I'm the man of the house when he's not here and it's my job to protect what's mine. That's my sister standing there that the animal violated, take a good look at her face again, ma,"

"Devon, honey, do you understand how it would hurt your father if you were to wind up in jail, do you? Give me the gun, baby before somebody get's hurt." He ignored Evelyn and instead walked back over to where Sissy stood. He looked at her face carefully, memorizing every scratch, bump, cut and bruise. Putting his fist in his mouth to keep from yelling, he asked her, pitifully,

"Sissy..did he..did he. Awh, Lawd" Sissy pulled her brother to her and hugged him tightly,

"Devon, I'll go away, please, ya'aw can send me away, I'll go away. Please don't, Devon, I love you, I don't wan'chew ta go ta jail on'a count 'a me," He hugged her and then pushed her away,

"It won't be on'a count'a you, and you remember dat. He's the monster, not you,"Devon said, sternly.

"Devon, listen, okay, we can call the police, let them take care of this," Evelyn pleaded.

"Oh, now dat's a good idea, the police. Now, what da hell dey gon' do? Dey ain't neva' cared about us hurtin' one another, less black folks dey got'ta do in, and put in jail. Unless she dead dey don't give a damn, 'n even den' dey gon' say dey can't fin'im. I know what's happenin' out der, ma. It ain't goin' down like 'dat wit' Sissy." With that he headed for the back door. They both knew what could happen if he got outta the house.

When he attempted to pass Evelyn, on his way to the back door, she surprised him, throwing out her arm to block him. With his massive size and well toned muscles, carefully choreographed at the gym, he simply brushed past Evelyn' arm as if it were an insignificant twig. Sissy sprung into action, by running and grabbing him around his waist. With all of her one hundred and sixteen pounds, having the benefit of the element of surprise to her advantage, she dropped to the floor, pulling hard , she brought him down. He angrily tried prying her hands loose,

"Don't let go, Sissy," Evelyn ran up behind them. Sissy held on for dear life. Her mother began trying to pry his hand loose from the gun he embraced, as if it were a close friend. Evelyn clasped his wrist, risking getting shot herself, she didn't care, if it meant stopping Devon. She wouldn't have him spend one night in jail for the likes of Brandon Jones, "give it to me, Devon," she warned her son, her breathing becoming more and more labored. She gathered more strength from God knows where, and she pushed harder against the fingers that looked so much like her own. The madman's grip he had on the gun made if difficult, if not impossible, for her to move the fingers even an eighth of an inch, still, she and Sissy tried.

Both lay atop Devon as he tried to turn over, for he had no strength lying on his stomach. Holding onto his waist, Sissy increased the strength of her grasp and prayed to God. Hugging his waist even tighter as he turned over, but her grip began slipping and her brother easily stood up, working to shake each of them off his leg. Sissy hit him in the back of his knee in an attempt to make him loose his balance and fall, it failed. She jumped up and planned to jump on him again, this time, with more force. If she was going to fall then she would bring him down with her, offering her mother a better chance of wrestling the gun from his hand.

The struggle grew intense as did the sounds of the struggle. They almost had him down at one point, but the gun, pointed at his leg, afraid it may discharge, made them both loosen their grips,

"Mooo-ooove!" Devon screamed at them. Neither listened as Sissy slid down his leg, pulling her nail off at the quick.. Reaching towards his ankle he kept trying to shake her off. Evelyn took advantage of his preoccupation with Sissy and again tried to maneuver the gun from his hand. He just wouldn't let go. Evelyn put her foot between his feet and pushed on the right foot, causing him to loose his balance and fall. He stretched the gun towards the kitchen, falling on top of Sissy. At first none were aware that the gun had fallen from Devon's grasp, until he began pushing himself up, reaching for the gun. Evelyn jumped on top of him and reached for it also. All three pressed towards the gun, groaning and panting from the strain of the effort. Evelyn put her knee onto Devon's wrist, incapacitating his hand,

"Don't let him go, Sissy." Evelyn commanded. She stretched her body farther than she ever dreamed she could, her goal, the nozzle of the gun. His finger, right beside hers, fell short, her nails were longer, thank God for acrylic, she thought. Using the nail to simulate a hook ,she balanced the nozzle on the tip of her nail, until she was able to inch it a little closer. Slowly, she pulled it to her as Sissy placed her leg between Devon and the gun. At long last, Evelyn got her baby finger through the trigger and swooped the gun up. Quickly, jumping to her feet she moved away from Devon and ran towards the mud room. There she found a hammer. Cocking the gun to release the bullets, she took the hammer and beat the barrel until it was bent and useless.

Chapter Ten

The three of them somberly sat in the family room before a blazing fire, nobody spoke. Dinner, on hold, had been placed in the warming oven, indefinitely. Their appetites, disappeared along with their peace of mind. Lamont was extremely late coming home and hadn't phoned to say why. Sissy refused to go to the hospital to have herself examined and counseled by rape counselors.

Being a nurse, Evelyn knew exactly what to do to mend the bruises and the cuts, but didn't have a clue how to reclaim the lost pieces of Sissy's personality. Even though the ice pack she placed on Sissy's face would take some of the swelling down, it would be a few days before she would be presentable enough to return to school. It was all just too much for Evelyn to deal with. What began as a nice, relaxing evening at home, strangely turned into the saddest evening of her life.

Feeling she needed some measure of vindication for what Brandon did to her child, but against the advice of her children, Evelyn phoned the police. She pulled back the drapes and watched the two officers approach the house. Laughing amongst themselves about an inside joke, Evelyn knew immediately it had been a mistake to call them, but they were here. She ran and tried Lamont's cell again, no answer.

Opening the door for the two officers as she hung up the phone, she hadn't known exactly what to expect. Perhaps, some measure, however small, of sympathy for what Sissy had gone through was in order. What she got were two white officers who had no compassion or inclination of how a sensitive situation such as rape should be handled.

Breezing past her, hardly acknowledging her presence as she opened the door, the big fat, older officer, still smacking on his dinner, seemed upset that his meal had been interrupted. In a hurry to get the job done, he surveyed the house, visually inspecting every nook and cranny as he sized them up, surprised to find African Americans in such a posh environment. He pulled out the all important spiral pad upon which, he would condense an entire evening of hell onto one single sheet of paper, the size of Serrita's hand. She wondered how does one reduce the monumental pain of rape to ten lines on a sheet of notebook paper. The questioning began with basic information, but soon turned,

"..was the school locked at that time, how did he gain entry into the building?" the big officer swallowed the last remains of his meal, wiped his mouth on the back of his hand and continued.

"Pig." Evelyn thought to herself.

"All of the doors weren't locked, just the main entrance was locked, I really don't know, I guess dat's how he got in there.,"Sissy answered weakly, her head laid firmly on her brother's chest.

"Uh-huh, listen, tell me, was this a routine, had he picked you up before from school," the skinny officer asked, his question filled with innuendos.

"Yes..he'd picked me up before,"Sissy answered.

"So, he was picking you up like he'd done countless times before, is that right?" the big officer interjected. They planned to work her over as if they were questioning a murder suspect.

"Yes,"

"And the two of you, were you lovers? You were sexually active, right,"the big officer smirked.

"Uh, excuse me officer..I don't know your names, you never bothered to identify yourselves," Devon said in an irritated voice, "That questioning is out of line,"

"Well, son my business is with the young lady, not you, but my name is officer Sullivan and this is officer Campbell," the skinny officer replied rudely.

"Well, officers Sullivan and Campbell, we didn't call you here about a sexual assault, we called you here about a plan assault and battery. Can't you see that the guy beat my sister, look at her face. What difference does it make whether she was intimate with him or not, he still has no right to do this to her, look at her," Devon said angrily.

"I think you'd better calm down so that we can get the facts straight. It's quite possible this could've been a lover's quarrel," the big officer warned.

"A lover's quarrel! Are you crazy! Is this the way you quarrel with your wife, man, this is crazy," Devon yelled, easing himself up off the sofa.

"Well, it is her word against his, there were no witnesses, and I'm gonna have to ask you to sit down young man," The big officer warned again, motioning for Devon to sit back down. Devon left the room but not before he said,

"Listen, officers, I'm in my own house, breaking no laws, I can get up and down, walk anywhere I want to, I'm not intimidated by you, just do your job, man," Devon turned to Evelyn and said sadly, "So much for the great idea of bringing the police in on this, ma.. You should've let me handle it my way. They don't care about her or us."Devon turned and ran up the stairs slamming his bedroom door behind him.

"Officer are you telling me that my daughter gets beaten like this and there's nothing you can do about it," Evelyn asked.

"We'll go back to the station and make out a report, but I can just tell you that not a lot will come out of this. It happened on school property and the best thing might be to pursue it through the administrators. I'm sorry to inform you that this young man is no stranger to the precinct, he's done this before and will do it again. He knows how to stay, if only a fraction, inside the line of the law. I would suggest at least taking out a restraining order. Still I have ta tell ya', based on what I've seen of him in the past, he has no respect for restraining orders. It just puts everybody on notice, in the event things take a turn for the worse," the skinny officer informed them.

"If you would just consider going into emergency and making out a report, we'd have more to work with, okay. Call us if you need us, we truly are sorry for your pain, Ms. Hill. Take care." the big officer said as the voice of their dispatcher came over their radios, calling them to their next victim.

Evelyn, studied the ketchup stained shirt Officer Campbell wore, his pot belly hanging just below the stainless steel buckle encrusted with the city's emblem on it. His breathing, labored, as little beads of sweat formed on is forehead, and as his face flushed beet red, she recognized useless when she saw it.

With the help of pain medication, hot tea and a warm alcohol bath, Sissy finally fell off to sleep in Evelyn's bed, refusing to sleep in her own room. Evelyn peeked out her door to see if the light was on in Devon's room, it was, he was studying for the mid-term he had the following day. Evelyn grabbed her coat, her keys, and snuck out the back door

Sitting outside Denise's house, her vintage Jag's engine still running, Evelyn tried Lamont's cell again, no answer. She had to hurry in case Sissy awakened, she wanted to be there. Throwing her one-hundred percent cashmere cape about her, she stepped out of her car and into the nippiness of the evening. With spring fast approaching, Cleveland's daytime weather, mostly mild, with a persistent overcast. At night, often capped off as low as seventeen degrees Farenheight. Looking up to the heavens, the sunset long gone, strangely it was the stars, whose names she couldn't remember, that offered her comfort. She rang Denise's doorbell and waited,

"Mrs. Hill, hay. Sissy isn't here,"Denise said, puzzled.

"Get your coat, sweety, I need you to go with me somewhere..Oh, hi Betty, how've you been,"she didn't know Denise's mother, Betty was standing behind the door. People hated the way she often surprised you that way, "creeping" as most would describe it. Usually like clock-work Betty was asleep by this time of night, but because she needed her to be asleep, of course she wasn't.

"Fine, Evelyn, how you been, gurl. Come on in. Denise, don't just have her standing outside like that." Inside, Evelyn could smell the butter and eggs from the pound cake baking in Betty's oven and any other time she would've taken off her coat and had a piece, along with some of Betty's specially brewed coffee. Tonight however, coffee and pound cake were the furthest thing from her mind.

"Denise I need you to help me pick out a gift for Sissy, can you do..do that honey,"she stumbled over the lie.

"What's the special occassion, it's not her birthday, cause I know her.." Betty butted in. Evelyn was impatient with her inquiry. As much time as her daughter spent at their house she felt offended she would question her this way.

"Well, Sissy received the presidential scholarship from Tuskegee University and girl you know I have to get that girl something special, I want Denise to help pick it out, can you," she turned to Denise. Denise, very perceptive, she knew it was all a lie.

"We were going over to my mother's to take the cake when it's done, but you can just drop her there afterwards if that's okay," Betty said.

"Perfect," Evelyn put on her phoniest of smiles, "Come on sweety, I don't want to keep you too long."

Inside the car she turned to Denise and revealed the real reason for her visit,

"Denise, show me where that animal lives. He almost killed Sissy today..and don't tell me you don't know, I happen to know that you do,"Evelyn said not moving her lips as she waved good-bye to Betty.

"Turn around and head back towards Lee. Is she okay," Denise asked, apprehensively.

"Barely, he raped her too,"Evelyn sucked in the words, which helped her to hold back her tears.

"Where,"Denise asked.

"At the school, this afternoon,"

"Oh yeah, perfect time, everybody was gone down to finals, son of a bitch,"

"Yeah, she stayed after school to help Justin, you remember him, the football player, Justin.

"Oh yeah,"

"Well, he jumped on her for being with Justin alone, said she was screwin'im. He went crazy Neicey and he messed her face up,"

"Oh my God, Mrs. Hill she don't listen to me when I tried to tell her to get away from'im. I'm so scared. You don't know'im Mrs. Hill, he's packin',"

"If he uses it on me tonight, cause I 'm gonna make'im mad, you take the car and go back to your house. I can't just let him do this to my daughter and not say a word,"

"I understand, Mrs. Hill, be careful, he's dangerous." They drove in silence the rest of the way.

She pulled in front of the little, white bungalow with it's peeling paint, littered lawn and huge patches of dirt for lawn, and turned off the engine of the car. She knew he was home, his car sat parked in the driveway. She forced herself out of the car, deciding to make up her speech as she went along, knowing that anything planned wouldn't make a bit of difference to him anyway.

She walked up the rickety steps and knocked on the finger smudged door,

"Who is it,"someone spoke cautiously from behind the door. She believed it to be Constance Jones, his mother.

"Mrs. Hill, Serrita Hill's mother, let me in please," she'd carefully calculated what it would take to get inside, appearing calm and reasonable, still, she heard Brandon say to his mother in a barely audible voice,

"Don't let her in, ma,"

"I ain't got nuttin' ta hide. Git'cho ass up from'der'n make yo'self presen'able, git up. What'da hell you done now," Finally, after much scuffling and rearranging behind the door, it was opened and Constance Jones stood poised in her too tight, vinyl jumpsuit, ready for a fight, "Anything wrong, Mrs. Hill?"

"Yeah, I want to see Brandon. Did he tell you how he jumped on my little girl today, how he messed her face up and raped her, did he tell you that," Evelyn asked sarcastically, as Brandon entered the room, a cold beer in his hand. Constance Jones turned and coldly stared at her son, which Evelyn mistakenly interpreted as a sign of support. Perhaps Constance has an aversion to abuse and would help me right this wrong, she thought. Wrong.

"How you gon' rape somebody dat gives you da pussy whenever you wants it, brings it ova' here willingly. I think you betta' rethink wha'chew sayin'. Brandon ain't gotta rape nobody, all da girls calling here, why he gotta rape yo' litt'l darlin', huh, tell me, why? My advice to you is ta keep her at home and ya ain't gotta worry'bout her gettin' her ass whupped. I don't mean no harm but da truth is da light, I say. Every time I turn'round she here. Don't ask me ta solve yo' problems, Mrs. Hill, you gotta solve'em yo'self. She comes ta my house, I can't stop her, you gotta stop her. It's her two feet what brings her here, remember 'dat," Constance said, the words stinging Evelyn like a nest of angry wasps.

"He did this at the high-school..Mrs. Jones, I'd like to have a few words with Brandon alone, we need to get some things straight, he and I," Evelyn said.

"I ain't got no problem wit' you talkin' to'im but make sho' you don't disturb nothin' in my house, it may not be Shaker Heights but I worked fo' it," Constance smirked.

"Of course," Evelyn said looking around the disheveled living room with it's stained carpet, torn curtains and piles of dirty clothes on the sofa. With that Constance turned and left by the front door to a waiting, old cadillac, parked in front of the house, a man sat inside the running car.

Brandon sat awkwardly alongside the pile of dirty clothes, nursing his beer. Evelyn shook, finally, coming face to face with the monster who'd beat her daughter down, like a helpless animal.

"You got another," she motioned for a beer, waiting for some of the anger to leave her body, enabling her to speak legibly. Still, her thoughts turned sinister, with just the two of them in the house she thought of the many ways she could kill him, just do away with this annoying problem he'd forced on them. He came back into the living room, handing her the beer without opening it. "That figures," she thought. She popped the tab and took a big pull from the can. Wiping her mouth as some spilled over the sides from drinking too fast, she began,

"You think you a big man, beatin' up on little girls, don't you," she said nastily, taking a seat across from him without being offered. A sharp spring from the ancient loveseat plunged right into the crease of her buttocks, not even flinching, she felt no pain, it was a minor inconvenience compared to what her daughter lived through.

What she really wanted to do was get up and beat him senseless. Not only did she want to beat him, she imagined the feeling of utter joy, as she scratched his flawless, chocolate skin and bit into his flesh, tearing out his flesh and chewing the chunks, spitting the remains into a blazing fire. He was disgusting, sitting there, dressed in expensive designer clothes in such a nasty house. At that moment she felt hatred, or something beyond, in a place she'd never traveled to.

"You meddlin' in something, ain't none of yo' bu'ness," the ludicrous comment, a pathetic attempt at defending his behavior, only made Evelyn angrier.

"My daughter is my business, ass-hole. If you think, for one second that I'm going to sit idly by and watch you destroy her, then you're dumber than you look. She means everything to me, got that , everythang. I realize that you've got some issues here, you and your family, still it's no excuse, we all got issues, every family, but you work to overcome, not beat people up helpless young girls, threaten them with guns. Your intentions to bring Sissy down sucks, and it is a wimpy way of expressing the anger you feel. Now, you're sitting there thinking to yourself, who the hell does she think she is comin' in here talking to me this way, I'm a bad nigga and I'll do..well Brandon what will you do? Wha'chew gon' do, Brandon..shoot us all? I know about your little threats, heard'em all. You can't hold on to her unless you threaten her brother with a gun, huh, big man. You know she'd do anything to protect him, even lay down her life, so you'll use her love for her brother. What a scuzzy thing to do, you can't hold on to her any other way, can ya?" she yelled. He made a move to get up from the sofa, but not before she detected the absence of life in his cold, empty eyes, "Sit down, dammit, sit down while I'm speaking to you, that's the very least you owe me after what you've done to my daughter," she screamed,

"Well if you think I did something to your family, then call the police, but leave me da hell alone," he replied.

"Leave you alone? Leave you alone," she hissed, "why I'd love to leave you alone, but as it stands, you're forcing yourself on me. Do you think Sissy would be with a looser like you if you weren't threatening her..

scaring her into being with you, we both know she would not. Brandon, she has plans for herself, but then that's the problem isn't it, they don't include you, do they? Listen Brandon, you're not going to bring my husband or my son down with you, I've checked, that's your M.O. You usually threaten the family, try to scare them too, thinking they'll just sit by and let you have your way. But in my case, no, neither one of them, my husband or my son will be involved in this, okay. No, this is between you and me. If it's a family feud you want then that's what you'll get, only thing, there's only one rule, I'm the only participant. Remember, now, you got a family too and I suppose you like them, cause you don't know what love is.." Evelyn stood up,

"..I have a motto, Brandon, if you can't beat'em, then join'em. I'll take you outta here before I let you destroy my baby, either one of them. Don't mess wit' me," she walked over to Brandon, got up in his face and eyeballed him, "You hurt her again, or any of my family and I will hunt you down like an animal. I will give up everything I have, sell everything I got, to find you, you will not escape my wrath. I can be relentless, I'm willing to die for her. I'm sure you hadn't counted on that one. Put your hands on her again.. you will be sorry," she lowered her voice, "Remember sweety, you've got a family too and baby, if I lose any one of mine, you'll lose one of yours, tit for tat, got it. Sissy may feel helpless, but Mommy don't. You're not the only person who can go out and get a gun, we all have that right. I can get one too, remember that. I got something fo' yo' ass and Mommy won't hesitate to use it." She said finally, backing away from him, patting her empty coach purse, admitting to herself , the threats were idle, just talk, she could never kill.

Outside, Evelyn closed the door and leaned against it, hyperventilating. In a million years she would never have dreamed she'd find herself in such a mess. Hurrying back to the car, she realized she still hadn't heard from Lamont, it was just one more thing for her to worry about., she sighed. Life had become about as complicated as she'd ever seen it.

Pulling into her driveway, after dropping Denise at her grandmother's, she searched for his car and still, no Lamont in sight. When she reached for the handle to the screen door, Devon met her at the door,

"Ma, Dad is sick, he's in emergency."

Chapter Eleven

"Honey da Lawd ain't gon' put mo' on ya den you kin bear, I declare he won't." Mrs. Walker proclaimed in that sing song way of hers,

"You have my prayers, Sistah Hill," another church member filed by Evelyn's chair, which had been placed in the middle of her bay window, like a thrown, by her well intentioned mother, Ms. Ida Mae. There Evelyn sat, alone, as if she were a queen they'd all come to pay ohmage to. Still existing in a cocoon of denial, with the residuals of death clawing away at her protective cocoon, scraping it away, piece by piece, leaving her helpless and exposed.

Taking more time for her, as she'd never gone through this sort of thing before, except with her grandparents. She remembered her grandmother's cold, lifeless body, dressed in her "good suit", stretched across the living room of the old house back on the farm in Georgia. Knowing that her beloved Nana lay only a few feet away, as if sleeping, she remembered trying to talk to her. When Nana didn't respond , with no adults around, she'd crawled inside the casket and decided to take a nap with her. Later when Ms. Ida Mae found Evelyn sleeping beside the dead body, she never forgot her mother's shrilled cries, believing that her daughter was marked for death as a result of having laid down inside the casket. She hadn't been able to sleep at all that night, nor would she be able to tonight. She'd never slept without her man before, ever.

"I'm so sorry to hear about Lamont, Evelyn, let me know if there is anything I can do fo' ya honey, just call and I'm here." Another one of Ms. Ida's friends, filed by and attempted to pick up her limp, clammy hand, dead it felt, just like her man.

"Trust God in his infinite wisdom, Evelyn. He knows what's best fo' us," she didn't know the person speaking or what the hell they meant, but their bad breath would be forever embedded in her memory. She didn't know how much longer she could take hearing the empty quotes, spoken out of duty and not love. She felt sick. The house was filled to capacity with curiosity seekers, a few love ones and a sprinkle of real friends. She wanted them all to go, except for, Lisa.

She didn't even have the opportunity to say good-by to him, his heart just gave out without a moment's notice, it was that simple. By the time she and Devon reached the hospital that night, he was gone. She stood looking down at his still body and thought about the last time they'd made love. Strangely, it crossed her mind to just mount him, lay on top of him, even though lifeless, she climbed onto the cold, steel gurney and lay on her husbands body, still warm. She laid there, in an effort to suck out any particles of love or life which may have lingered behind, like the fish who's head she chopped off, still, wreathing around in the sink, until the last remaining particles of life disappated, realizing the head would not be reattached, then ceased swarming around inside. She would draw these small particles of life into her body and just maybe she could feel normal.

"I'm getting ready to put all the food away, so these people will leave, you want anything before I do," Her buddy, Lisa whispered in her ear.

"Please get them out of here. You're staying, right,"

"Right." Lisa said, moving quickly to get all the food wrapped, placed into containers and into the fridge. After kissing her on the cheek, Mike gathered up he and Lisa's four boys and headed for home. Evelyn recognized the absence of emotion in Mike's eyes and knew the pain of loosing his best friend suddenly this way, would come crashing down on him like a semi. She wondered, where he would be when it happened.

"I'm taking her upstairs, y'aw. Everybody say your good nights, my sistah is goin'ta bed, at leas'fo a nap," It was Juney, Lamont's baby brother helping her up. Ms. Ida Mae, her sister, Valerie and Juney all supported her over to the stairs, assisting her as if she were a paraplathegic and they, physical therapists. With everyone tip-toeing around her, walking on eggshells this way, she was evolving into the fragile soul they were turning her into. She'd begun to shuffle along like the doped up patients in the psych ward at the hospital where she worked, somberly complacent and satisfied to have others do all their thinking for them.

"Valerie, go'head 'n turn down yo' sister's bed, so it's ready when she gits up 'der," Ms. Ida Mae ordered.

"Kay, Ma," Valerie left the huddle of support and ran ahead.

"I already turn't it down, Ms. Ida," Evelyn's father yelled from upstairs. A traffic jam ensued on the stairwell, as everybody jammed up there, all wanting to help her to bed. Eager to get her settled and out of sight, figuring once she was bedded down, they wouldn't have to see the pitiful expression of abandonment on her face. Putting her to bed offered them too, the opportunity to rest, and to not have to be on point every second, watching and wondering, should they say this or should they do that, should they mention Lamont's name, should they not.

Immediately she recognized the comfort the privacy of her bedroom brought to her. The smell of him was everywhere and she wanted to bask in it for a while.

"Kay, everybody out, I'm gon' talk to sis for a minute and then I'm gon' leave too. We haven't talked at all today," Juney said, pulling the covers up around her.

"Take care of her, Juney, my baby been through hell,"Ms. Ida said, sadly as she headed for the door.

"I know, Ms. Ida." He kissed Ms. Ida and saw her to the door. Evelyn looked out of her bedroom window at the night. The sound of singing crickets and an ambulance siren in the distance were the only signs of life.

She studied Juney, as he closed the door and thought how much like Lamont he looked. For a second she pretended he was Lamont, and that everything was normal, that it was Lamont closing the door and securing the house for the night. She imagined him coming to bed with a good book, she with her own book, as they both read quietly, occassionally looking into each other's eyes, each giving the other a smile of love and friendship. That kind of peace, now, lost to her forever.

"You look just like your brother, you know that," she smiled as the tears slid down her face.

"You okay wit' dat, sis,"

"Of course I am,"

"You know I was 'da one s'pose ta marry you anyway, I'm still mad 'bout dat," Juney smiled weakly. He picked up her hand and looked into her eyes. That's where the familiarity to his brother ended, Juney's touch, different from Lamont's, ended the pretense,

"Sis, I'm here fo' you. You and da kids, you're my responsibility now. I know my brotha, he was a smart, intelligent man, so I know he left you well provided fo', dat I ain't gotta worry'bout. Sis, you know I live my life in da streets, I heard some things'bout my niece. I couldn't leave her' without finding out whaz goin' down," God bless'im, she thought.

Juney, the black sheep of the family, who's job status, permanently unclear, never took up with conventional living or obligating himself to a nine to five. Shunning the conformist's lifestyle, he lived on the edge of life. Most people, while unsure of Juney's method of hustle, loved him in spite of and some because of the excitement surrounding him. Draped in a butter soft, leather suit, a Rolex watch hanging from his wrist, accessorized by the appropiate bling-bling, Juney rolled like the royalty of hustlers.

"Step over to the window, Juney," Evelyn nodded towards the window. He got up and cautiously approached the window, standing off to the side instead of the front. Making this move with the practiced expertise of a person from the underworld, once there, he peeked out, from the right side first, and then the left. Some of the guests from downstairs were milling about in the street, getting into their cars, strapping small children into car seats, neighbors walked to their respective homes, nothing unusual,

"Jus' some folks pushin' up outta here..talk to me,"he said, still watching.

"There's an old restored, red, fifty-seven Chevy out there..see it," she said pointedly.

"Kay..who's da nigga sittin' in der,"

"Sissy's boyfriend..he beats her, but then you already know that, right,"

" Hear say, I needed ta confirm it,"

" The fact that Sissy is grieving for her father means nothing to him,"she explained.

"Ain't no problem, we can fix dis shit. Did my brother know anything'bout dis,"

"It's ironic, I worked so hard to keep it from him, afraid it might kill'im and now.."her voice, trailed off.

"I already checked out da situation..learned some interesting stuff 'bout dis cat. His name is Brandon, right," he still kept an eye on the car.

"Right,"

"His ole man used to whup on da momma, when dey was ta'getha. He needed her ta git out der 'n git dat smack fo'im, he had about a two-hundred dollar a day habit. He used ta beat da hell out'da kids too..it was a bad scene, man. Da best thing dat ever happen to'em is when dat nigga got da hell on up outta der. One 'a two things we can do here..we can arrange fo' im to git da ass whuppin' of his life..confine 'im to a hospital bed for a minute, nobody gotta know," he whispered, "or, we can make da solution..final, you follow me,."He stared at her, watching her carefully to see if she understood the implications behind the term, "final."

She took a cold hard look at the options he laid before her and wondered if she'd done the right thing by telling Juney. Raised to be a survivor, still she knew nothing about the streets. The closest her parents' ever came to abuse during an argument was, raising their voices an octave level or two. When angry, going to their respective corners of the house, to cool down, was the way anger was handled in her parent's as well as her house. Bringing the argument to a close in a dignified manner consisted of Ms. Ida fixing her Dad's favorite meal, or her Dad would bring the clothes in off the line for her mother, that's the kind of arguing she was used to.

"I know somebody dat will deal wit' dis fo' us.. I know people, Evelyn. It will be quick and clean,"he said finally.

"Juney, no. As much as I would love to, that just doesn't sit well with me..who is this person,"she asked in spite of herself.

"No..we nev'a want to know a name, nev'a. He handles del'cate matters like dis. We ain't got many choices here sis, I say we put dis cat, flat out, end da drama, he's trouble,"

"Juney.." Evelyn looked around the room making sure nobody lurked around a closed door or in a corner of the closet, "are you suggesting that we..I can't even say it, Juney..kill him,"

"Exac'ly what I'm sayin'," he whispered, unwavering in his conviction.

"It's a bad situation, but I could never be a party to someone's death. That would make me just as bad a person as he is,"

"Kay then, you can be a good person wit' good intentions and a dead daughter, 'cause make no mistake, sis, keep foolin'round wit' dis cat, history tells me he'll take her outta here, take it to da bank and deposit dat shit,"

"Juney, I couldn't live with myself," her conviction, weakening each time Sissy face flashed before her eyes.

"Don't decide right now, I'm going to make contact jus' so I have my shit lined up," he picked up the phone and dialed the number of the anonimus person. She found it amazing that, by just picking up the phone and dialing a few numbers this faceless entity, completely unknown to her, would beat people up, hosptitalize them and even kill for you. Evelyn almost laughed at the obsurdity of it all.

"Sup, dis here is Juney, I need to rap wit'chew 'bout somethin', dawg. You got da 911, I'll holla at'cha later." Juney spoke to the answering machine of the anonymous person. As he hung up the phone he reached inside his wallet and handed her the person's card.

The card simply read, consulting agency, no name or address on the card, only two phone numbers. Evelyn threw the card into her night stand drawer, thinking she'd throw it out after Juney left. But after Juney left, tired from the days events, she fell fast asleep.

After kissing all the women and sisters from the church, shaking the hands with the men and saying his good-byes for the evening, Juney slipped into his silk Armante' jacket. Closing the door to his dead brother's house, he lit a cigarette and inhaled deeply. It had been more difficult than he imagined, to see his brother lowered into the ground that way, knowing he would never see him again. The finality of it took his breath away and he fought hard to hold back the tears. Equally hurting him, was this asshole disrespecting his brother's family this way, hanging out here during their time of grieving. He had to check this cat, couldn't let him disrespect his family this way.

He removed his jewelry, carefully placing it in the safe he had installed inside his pearl white Escalade. He carefully stuffed his piece down inside his pants around the small of his back. He walked to the end of the driveway, buttoned his jacket, and looked unassumingly down the street, to see if the car was still there. "Dis asshole still sittin' der," he observed. He'd just scare the hell out of him, pistol whup'im for right now, he had other plans for him later, after all he was nothing, going around beating up on defenseless females, all his manhood wrapped up in controlling her. Juney knew his kind, had seen many of them in the streets, always avoiding a challenge with a man, unless they had a death wish. Nobody was going to treat his little niece that way and get away with it. He remembered her cute little face when she was a baby with only two front teeth, he'd bounce her up and down on his knee, and he loved the way she smelled of fresh baby powder.

Juney's life of crime spanned some twenty years. He dabbled in many things, from petty theft to grand larceny, a few cons here and there, mostly dealing in drugs. Not proud of what he did, hiding it well from his proud parents and older brothers who'd all managed to get an education and legitimate careers. Finding out too late in life about his dyslexia, Juney did the best he could. His goal in life had not been to deal drugs but the idea of living a mediocre existence, or in poverty had no appeal for him.

Juney walked around the corner first, in the opposite direction, he would circle back coming up from behind Brandon's car. He banked on Brandon's car door being unlocked, if it wasn't he would simply break his window out. He didn't want to do that, too much noise.

Hiding behind a massive group of bushes on the corner lot, Juney peeked around the bushes making sure he was still there listening to seventies cuts on his CD player. Slumped down in the front seat he appeared to be half asleep. It was then that Juney inhaled the sweet aroma of reefer, he smiled as thought, good he's high, dis outta really mess his ass up.

Running close to the ground, keeping himself lower than the car fender he crept up beside the driver side door and snatched it open,

"Pretty boy, Brandon. Whaddup,whaddup. Sup, dawg. What's da problem, you ain't got nothing else ta do but sit out here and guard my brother's house? Who asked you ta guard my brother's house Brandon," Falling out of the car when the door was suddenly snatched open, Brandon fell to the ground on his back with his legs still hanging from the seat, looking as if he were waiting on a diaper change. Juney put his size ten Italian leather boots in Brandon's chest, dead center and pressed down attempting to break his sternum. Brandon screamed,

"What da..hell! Git off me, git off me dawg or I'll.."Brandon threatened.

"..Or else you'll do what partna..wha'chew gon' do, beat my ass like you did my niece's, you sorry motha fucka.. Now shut da hell up and stop actin' like a little bitch, shut up." Juney reached around his back, feeling for his piece and pulled it out. He stuck the nozzle of his brand new colt forty-five semi-automatic up Brandon's left nostril and cocked it,

"Man wha'chew doing! I ain't did nothin' ta you! Who da hell are you,"beads of sweat broke out on his forehead, multiplying profusely.

"Wrong. Ya did do something ta me. You put yo' hands on my niece, I understands it's a regular thang that you do..beat her up I mean. Well, guess what? Tonight you will get a taste of what it feels like to be violated by someone fo' no reason, you follow me. First mistake Brandon, always investigate your victim's family and make sure dey don't have no crazy uncle in da family like me,"Juney laughed, he hadn't had this much fun since him and his brothers jumped on the Nelson brothers back in the day, in their old neighborhood.

"I'm jus' waitin' fo' somebody, I ain't did nothin' ta nobody.." the punk lied.

"I asked you, do you know what it feels like to get yo' ass whupped fo' no apparent reason.. answer me,"Juney kicked him in his lower jaw, forcing him to bite down on his tongue, real hard. Brandon suppressed a scream, but couldn't help moaning from the pain. Juney turned the forty-five around, held the nozzle between his forefinger and thumb and pistol whipped Brandon about the head and face with the shiny, new steal plated butt of the gun. With blood dripping from every crevice on his face, the punk had the nerve to beg for mercy.

"Get up, get up and get back in da damn car, get up in der,"Juney held the gun to his head as he got himself situated inside the car. He continued to hold it there as he spoke,

"Now, you git yo ass outta here and I don't ever want you 'round Sissy again, you got dat,"

"Word." Brandon shivered from the pain and humiliation.

"Now git'da hell on up outta here fo' I wipe dis ground up wit' cho dusty ass. Git outta here, you make me sick.." Brandon, weak, barely able to move, finally started the engine and drove away, slumped over the wheel, blood dripping all over the interior of his prized fifty-seven Chevy. Juney hoped his ass would crash into something, saving him the trouble of having to put him under later. As Brandon drove away, Juney picked up a rock from the nicely landscape arrangement in one of the neighbor's yard, and threw it at the back window of the fifty-seven Chevy, shattering it to pieces. Juney laughed to himself. The next week, Juney was busted for distribution.

Chapter Twelve

The incessant ringing of the telephone startled Evelyn, and when she glanced over at her clock it was only three in the morning. The first thing that came to mind, was, it might be Brandon calling, he had that kind of nerve. She eased the receiver out of it's cradle, not saying a word, she listened, she'd let him speak first.

"This here is Mighty. Somebody called me from this number,"the stranger asked guardedly. Evelyn, not fully awake, was annoyed with this "Mighty" for calling her house at this hour.

"What does he mean did somebody call him from this number," she thought, he just needs to ask for who he wants to speak with. Suddenly, the conversation between her and Juney rolled back through her mind. She imagined Juney as he stood by her bedside the night before, with the phone in his hand, speaking very calmly about, as Juney put it, flattening the cat out. The phone call she remembered, Juney made from her house and instinct told her the two calls were connected.

"Oh, yeah, I'm sorry, I think you want Juney or Julius," she kicked herself for revealing Juney's real name. She recalled him saying, "we neva want ta know names, neva,"

"Yeah, I know'em, is he there,"the stranger asked.

"No, no he was here earlier, but he left,"she said, trying to sound as pleasant as possible at three o'clock in the morning. Why is he calling people, this time of night, she thought.

"Oh,"the stranger lingered as if trying to decide what to do next. Sleepy, she wanted to end the bizarre phone call and go back to sleep.

"Well, I'm sorry but I don't have a forwarding number for Juney,"she lied,

"No problem, I know how to get a hold of'im, peace,"he abruptly hung up the phone. Evelyn wasted no time thinking about the faceless caller. Her only concern at this point was the empty spot in her bed where Lamont used to be. She turned her back to the spot and concentrated on falling back to sleep.

The next day while taking an extra long time to slurp her luke warm coffee, having sent Lisa home to her family, she sat planning the remainder of her life. Impulsivity, in the past had never been a part of her strategy, but having played it safe her entire life, she felt the urge to take a leap of faith. Her husband, God bless his soul, left her well off. He made sure everything was paid in full, the house, their cars. After which, with hundreds of thousands of dollars to collect from insurance policies, she would be, according to some people's standards, rich. Not Oprah rich, but satisfied.

So, today she'd decided to make a clean break from her job as the head nurse of the geriatric unit at Saint Lukes Hospital. Her mission, to dive feet first into interior design on a full-time basis, it was her first love, her passion. Now that she could afford to do whatever she wanted with her life, she prepared to make major changes to it, beginning with her job at the hospital.

When she walked into the lobby of the hospital she felt regret for what she was about to do. Already understaffed, her abrupt departure would leave them scraping and hustling for a replacement. Still, she felt something pushing her forward, she needed this.

"Is Mrs. Mayer in, Susie," she asked her supervisor's secretary. Susie, a homely looking grandmother of two. Her piercing, cold blue eyes appeared awkward next to hair bleached too regularly, it looked like a blonde brillo soap pad. Poor Susie, who's husband recently left her, really had no life outside that of secretary. Because of her loyalty to her position, one would think she would be the best at her job, but she wasn't. Constantly botching simple, mundane jobs, somehow she'd remained in the position for more than twenty years. Susie's main interest was in telling people Mrs. Mayer couldn't see them without an appointment. Proudly she sat at her treasured post, in all her incompetent glory, as if guarding the queen of England herself.

"She'll be right back, Evelyn. You want to have a seat?" Susie said. She opened her desk drawer, pulled out an envelope and handed it to Evelyn, "This is for you, from all the staff over in the peds unit and the administration office. We cannot tell you how sorry we were to hear about Lamont," Evelyn accepted the card appreciatively, pushing the thought from her mind to check Susie for calling Lamont by his first name. She didn't even know Susie's used to be husband's first name, and even if she did, she wouldn't have used it, because she didn't know him like that.

"Thank you Susie," she said. At that moment, Mrs. Mayer returned to the office,

"Evelyn, dear, come in, have a seat in my office. I'll be right with you."Mrs. Mayer said compassionately. Evelyn took a seat in her office and sat looking at the family photo proudly displayed on her desk. The whole family positioned at accurate levels, were truly a good sample of Mrs. Mayer's perfect life. At least that's how she portrayed herself. According to Mrs. Mayer, Kathy, her name, none had a life as perfect as hers. Strutting around in a perfect size six body, kept that way, according to staff members, by regularly relieving herself after meals. She claimed to have the perfect husband, who absolutely loved what she did for him in bed. Rumor had it that the perfect husband, Paul, screwed anything in a skirt, that hadn't been dead more than twenty four hours. Her perfect four kids with their obsession for wearing the color black, were often picked up for drug possession. Still, whenever anybody asked Mrs. Mayer how life was treating her, she always answered, perfect,

"Susie, get Mr. Kaplan on the phone, Mrs. Stewart called in sick and he said earlier he'd cover for her," Mrs. Mayer said as she replaced an employee file into the cabinet.. Evelyn felt like a heel for what she was about to do.

"Evelyn, how are you making out since the passing of Mr. Hill," Mrs. Mayer asked, truly concerned. Evelyn wanted to scream, oh I'm just peachy since my whole world's been turned upside down, instead she replied,

"Well, I take it one day at a time, Mrs. Mayer," she wanted to get this over with, not carry on a friendly conversation about her loneliness.

"Now, you just take as much time as you need, honey. I know it's hard,"

"About the time, that's sort of why I'm here, Mrs. Mayer. I've decided not to return to work, I won't be coming back to work," you could've bit Mrs. Mayer in the ass, she was so stunned,

"I know you probably feel that way right now, it's not unusual, Evelyn, but give yourself some time to heal."Mrs. Mayer interjected her ten years spent as a psychiatric nurse into the conversation.

"No, Mrs. Mayer time won't heal this,"

"Well, Evelyn I don't understand, you're just going to give up your career? I know you like to dabble in interior design, but making a living doing that won't be easy, Evelyn, trust me." Mrs. Mayer tried to suppress her annoyance with Evelyn. But, she couldn't hide the subliminal suggestion, which hung in the air between them, that Evelyn didn't have sense enough to know what to do with her life. Besides, judging from the dinner parties she attended at Mrs. Mayer's big mansion in the suburbs , she truly didn't know anything about interior design.

"I've enjoyed working here, with you and the staff, Mrs. Mayer, you guys are like family to me,"she lied, "I'll stop in from time to time and check on you guys,"

With that, Evelyn shook the hand of a mouth wide opened, stunned, Mrs. Mayer, who's hand felt cold, and with no substance to them, were as weightless as air.

Later on that day, driving around mindlessly, no particular destination in mind, she stumbled upon exactly what she'd envisioned in her mind, but had not a clue how to find. She knew she'd done the right thing, leaving her job, when she stepped inside Goldstein and Goldstein Interiors. An establishment with a slightly Tuscan, Morrocan theme going on inside. Located on the pier section of downtown Cleveland, it was exactly the change she'd been looking for.

"May I help you," A cute blonde walked up to Evelyn and extended her hand.

"I would like to volunteer my services here in exchange for learning the business. Should I be speaking to you or someone else about this."Evelyn said, firmly.

"My name is Sandy and no, I'm not the person you need to speak with. You'll want to speak with Mr. Paul Goldstein Sr., he's the owner. Have a seat and let me see if he's available at this time, and if not we'll schedule you an appointment, how's that. Good luck." Evelyn instantly liked her.

Five minutes later Sandy returned with Mr. Goldstein. A slightly bent over, aging, but alert Jewish man, walked towards her, hopping from one foot to the other as if his feet hurt. The two of them sat amongst the beautiful furniture, plush pillows, sofas, antique wool rugs, hanging silk window dressings, the scent of lavender and old leather,

"What an unusual request, Mrs. Hill. I've never had anyone request such a thing and it is for that reason that I am considering it. Please, accept my condolences for the passing of your loved one. Death can be so mean, how it strips real love from our lives that way. I lost my parents during the Holocaust in Aushwitz. We were shipped there from Berlin, my mother, father, my brother and I. My father was a wealthy physician in Germany," he ended sadly.

"I'm so sorry, Mr. Goldstein,"she was afraid to ask about the brother for fear he might be dead.

"I know, life sucks sometimes doesn't it,"he searched her eyes.

"Yes it does."

"Awh, and who do we have here, Dad. Introduce me." A tall, dark, curly headed man walked up. Judging from looks alone, he had to be Mr. Goldstein's junior,

"Evelyn, he is what some would mistakenly call, the fruit of my loin, the apple of my eye, although I checked, there is no such thing as an apple in one's eye, or my prodigy, and that definition I'll accept because I'd like to believe there was some measure of intelligence passed along in the family gene pool. At the very least he is the person who stands to gain the most if I kill over right at this very moment, keep in mind, my son, that could all change by tomorrow. Quite simply put, this is my son, Paul. Now, you act nice Paul, I like her,"Mr. Goldstein ordered, with a twinkle in his eyes.

"Dad, who me, I'm offended, you're so critical of everything I do,"Paul laughed.

“Well, somebody’s gotta stop you from making an ass of yourself. Anyway, this is Mrs. Hill, Evelyn Hill. Evelyn, call me Paul, we’ll see you Monday morning, right,” Goldstein Sr, asked.

“Bright and early, and thank you Mr. Goldstein.. I mean Paul, for allowing me this opportunity.”she nodded graciously.

“Listen, Evelyn I have many opportunities that I can offer as well. How about me telling you about them over dinner.”Junior Goldstein said, smacking his lips, ready ta chow down on some black bootey. She laughed to herself as she headed for the door.

Chapter Thirteen

Evelyn peered outside the window of Goldstein & Goldstein, watching Lake Erie. Huge boulders of frozen ice rammed against each other as the temperature dropped below zero. The heavy February snow, near blizzard affect or "white out" conditions as Clevelanders called it, made it impossible to see in front of yourself. If the weather continued getting worse she'd leave her car parked in the underground parking garage and take the rapid transit home.

Not very much was happening inside the design showroom anyway, with the extreme weather threatening to shut the town down, only two clients lingered inside, inquiring about the pieces Paul Junior brought back from India. The Senior Paul went home early and the Junior Paul, left that morning for Atlanta, on a buying trip. Only Evelyn, Sandy, Brian and Nancy remained.

"I think they're at it again," Sandy whispered, nodding her head in the direction of Paul Senior's office.

"Who? Oh, Mr. and Mrs. Nymphette? Is that who you're talking about," Evelyn laughed.

"Who else? Girl, I want those two busted. I'm still mad about the Schwartz job going to them, it's not fair, Evelyn," Sandy pouted, sitting atop Evelyn's desk.

"I know, you work hard, girl and I understand your frustration but be patient, God has a way of turning things around in your favor, when you least expect it,"

"Well, he's going to have to do a lot of turning, they've racked in more accounts then all of us combined," Sandy's gray eyes widened with that revelation.

"Kay, so it's true, but you have to admit they hustle for it. They get out there in the trenches and often bring the business in themselves, not waiting for accounts to be assigned to them. If I hadn't just started out and wasn't assigned to "Staging" we could team up and possibly give them a run for their money,"

"That would be nice wouldn't it? Will you listen at those two, listen, shh, shh," Sandy tip toed over and stood behind the closed door. They both heard the moaning and then bodies engaged in sex, pushing up against the door.

"Now, that's tacky, girl. What's wrong with Nancy," Evelyn shook her head.

"Well, now you see, that's part of the excitement, see, the possibility of getting caught, a lot of people like the danger. I've been caught a couple times myself, not here, mind you, but elsewhere," Sandy gave her a wicked grin.

"Noooo..you are so bad. Uh, excuse me but Sandy, somebody better do something, here comes Paul Senior.

What's he doing coming back here, I thought he left for the day,"Evelyn rose from her desk, not knowing who's job it should be to let the empty headed couple know that he'd returned.

"Ain't my job,"Sandy backed away from the door.

Paul Senior ran a tight ship. It had taken him forty years to build the business, done with careful planning, some unscrupulous business tactics, brown nosing, hard work and lots of networking, eventually winning him a five star nod. Very proud of his accomplishments, he allowed no one, not even Paul Junior to jeopardize his achievements. So, Evelyn, unsure what his feelings would be about Brian and Nancy, both married to other people, oddly somehow felt responsible. The phone rang and she grabbed it before Sandy could, happy for the distraction,

"Goldstein and Goldstein, Mrs. Hill speaking, may I help you,"she answered quickly, following Paul Senior with her eyes.

"Yea, this is Mr. Walker, over in Moreland Hills, I was suppose to receive the specs for my kitchen yesterday from Paul Junior and I'm wondering if they're ready, or.."Evelyn listened intently, not really hearing what he said, her interest was in the voice. Deje-vu took her around in circles and back again. Remembering this task had been assigned to her earlier and she'd forgotten all about it, she scrambled so no one would know of her neglect.

"Oh, yes Mr. Walker the specs are here. I was just about to phone you to set up a time for the review and sign off. Paul Junior is away on a buying trip, my name is Evelyn Hill, and if it's okay with you, I will bring them out to you,"she redeemed herself.

"Today,"he asked impatiently.

"Of course,"dammit she thought. She'd have to get out there in the storm. Cleveland's weather, unpredictable and strange, it might be that very little snow had fallen out where Mr. Walker lived, at least that's what she hoped for. She hurriedly wrote down the address, hung up the phone and began gathering her things. Sandy rushed over with her nosey self,

"Don't leave me here with them,"she insisted. I think they heard him, either that or Brian just got his rock off," Sandy laughed, fanning herself just thinking about it..

"His rock? Oh, them, I can't think about Nancy and Brian right now, I've gotta get out here in this blizzard and take these specs to a, Mr. Walker. You know'im,"

"That was him calling,"Sandy asked. Evelyn watched her closely, to see if her expression would give away her relationship with Mr. Walker. Having slept with a couple clients that Evelyn knew of, she wondered if Mr. Walker was one that she didn't know about. If Paul Senior ever found out he'd fire her, he strictly prohibited fratenizing with his clients.

"Yea, that was him calling.. shoot I had plans for this evening. You know'im,"

"Uh huh, I think I do..tall black guy," she hadn't slept with him, or else she was pretending. Anyway, why did she even care?

"I've never seen him up close before but, yea I think we're talking about the same person," Evelyn searched her desk for her car keys and put the directions inside her coat pocket, "I promised Paul Junior I'd handle this. He'll sit down later with Paul and make any corrections if any are needed. Although I can't see what the big rush is to have them today. What's the story on Mr. Walker," a strange feeling had come over when she heard his voice on the phone, as if she'd known him in another life or something, it was weird.

"Well, I'm not sure what his story is. Supposedly, he's a police detective or something. But when you see that house, I have been to the house, didn't see him though, it makes you wonder what kind of salaries detectives earn these days. Maybe I'm in the wrong business," Sandy said, regrettably.

"Kay, is that the real story, or is there another version?"

"Don't know. According to Paul Senior he made his fortune through stock investments. He and Paul Senior are very good friends, that's all I know. Anyway, long as he pays the bill we don't need to know the whole story, do we girl," Sandy said finally.

"I know that's right," Evelyn smiled as she headed for her car, "have a great weekend, girlfriend."she passed Paul Senior on his way into the store, "Good night Paul. I'm on my way over to Mr. Walker's, in Moreland Hills, I promised Paul Junior I'd handle this for him," Paul Senior winked, "I think you're a better person for the job than Paul Junior, anyway." They both laughed and she jumped into the Jag, started it up and got out to clean off the foot of snow piled on top of it.

Evelyn slid around the streets of Cleveland, speeding, trying to make time, so as not to get caught in the storm after dark. Just as she'd predicted, when she reached the other side of town, the snow barely covered the ground. With salt already applied to the streets she could drive normally.

She swung a right onto Brainard, heading for the posh Moreland Hills suburb of Cleveland, with it's unique mixture of contemporary mansions, traditional houses, french inspired exteriors, and scenic landscape designs. Covered in freshly fallen snow, its' picturesque appearance deserved to grace the front of a postcard.

Evelyn pulled the paper from her pocket, checking for the address and realized she'd already passed it. Turning around in the driveway of a stranger, landed her right in front of the house. She pulled into the driveway and turned off the engine of her car. Reaching over to the back seat, retrieving the architect's plans, she turned back around and found herself looking into the face of the most viscous looking Doberman she'd ever seen. A second or two could have meant the difference between her being inside her car looking out, or the dog tearing her flesh apart with teeth so sharp, they looked as if they'd been professionally sharpened, coming to jagged points like that of saw. She watched in horror as the dog barked loudly, pushing himself against the car, slobbering all over the driver side window. "Did he forget that I was coming?" she thought, her heart in her mouth.

"King! Get over here, git I say." A dark, handsome, well built prince, of a black man, jerked the front door open, and yelled to the dog, who quickly obeyed, running back around to the rear of the brick Georgian mansion, complete with pillars. The man motioned for Evelyn to pull into the three car garage next to a midnight blue Benz. A red truck stood parked farther down inside the garage, filled with tools, its' body dripping with melting snow.

"Mrs. Hill? Hey, I'm Mr. Walker, call me Blake,"he walked into the garage to help bring her things inside. He came off as friendly, but cautiously distinguished. For an instant, as the two shook hands, she thought she saw recognition in his eyes, perhaps from a previous meeting, but he didn't. When she looked into his eyes a second time, the emptiness of his gaze put a halt to the inquiry.

"Come inside and make yourself at home, please,"he offered, kindly, holding the door for her,

"Thank you. Need I ask, does your dog bite," Evelyn laughed nervously.

"Well, let's just say if he's prompted, he will. But a good rule of thumb to follow is, if an animal has teeth, than the potential for being bitten is there, you know what I mean,"he laughed.

"I know that's right, Mr. Walker,"she smiled.

"Call me Blake, please," He waited for her to offer him the same privilege, instead, she said nothing, "the reason I didn't have the dog secured..and I apologize for that, because he is scary if you don't know him. My mother just had emergency surgery and my brother called long distance to give me the report on her condition, probably just as you pulled up. I was talking on the phone and didn't hear the car,"he said apologetically, showing her to her seat.

"Please, don't apologize, it's all good. How's your mom doing? Is she going to be alright,"Evelyn tried to focus on the conversation but found it hard. The house, breathtakingly beautiful, hindered her ability to concentrate. Gleaming wood floors, expertly textured wall treatments, the arched ceilings and doorways, leaded glass windows, the hand crafted tiled fireplaces and the custom made furniture all provided a pretty accurate picture of the amount of money Mr. Walker was rolling with. She wondered how his story really read, who would the people that really knew him, say he was. He seemed just a little out of place in all the finery, fitting in more apropppiately in an urban environment, out in the trenches, with people, not in a such a secluded, uppity area as this. His hands, rough and scared were made for hard work and helping others. About six feet one, his handsome pecan colored face, inset with huge brown eyes, made more pronounced by a mere whisper of cold, black, wavy hair drew her in. Thick lips were accentuated by a nicely shaped go-tee.

Sitting there, in the cozy room by a warm fire, the environment seemed strangely familiar to her, even though she had never been there before, at least not in this lifetime. She tried to remember some of her recent dreams, perhaps the answer lie within one of her dreams.

"The specs?" she handed them to him. After all, that is the reason she'd come. For a minute they'd both forgotten the purpose of her visit.

"Right. Can I get you something to drink, some wine, while I look them over. I'm afraid I'm not being a very good host, let me have your coat,"he said. When she stood up to remove it, he walked up behind her to help. She felt his warm breath on her neck and enjoyed the sensation.

"Some wine would be nice, thank you,"not really sure drinking was appropiate at this time. What the heck, she thought, it was Friday.

"I'll be right back. Come over here and sit right by the fire, come on, I insist..warm up a little,"

"Well, okay but I won't be staying long.."her voice trailed off. She'd lost her mind, sitting up in this man's house, who she did not know, having a glass of wine with him no less. She didn't know anything about him except that he and Paul Senior were good friends. She trusted Paul enough to rely on his judgement.

"I didn't say how long you were staying, but while you are here, I want you to be comfortable, okay," he smiled.

"Kay,"she returned the smile and curled up on the massive, white shag rug that lay stretched out on the floor directly in front of the fire, just like at home. He returned, handing her the glass of wine,

"I also put the kettle on for tea, you like,"

"Um huh,"she searched for words, which strangely alluded her.

"Now, the specs. The reason that I had you come out here in weather like this, is because of the time crunch," he said.

"Time crunch?"she answered, perplexed. Perhaps he didn't understand, she was just an intern, he really didn't need to explain anything to her.

"Yea, see, I want to have my family reunion here at my house this summer and the kitchen, well you've seen it, needs help. If we don't begin the work in say, two weeks, which would make it March, they won't be finished by June. So, let's see what we have here." he unrolled the plans and headed back into the kitchen. Evelyn finished her wine, got up and went into the kitchen with Blake as he went over the plans.

"I thought I specifically told them that I didn't want the wall here, between the kitchen and the family room, I want it open.. otherwise I'm pleased,"he pointed out.

"That can very easily be changed, but let me just mark it at the bottom to alleviate confusion,"she marked the correction at the bottom and removed the whistling kettle from the stove. She rummaged around in the cabinets for the tea, took out a bag for each of them and poured the boiling water into their mugs, covering the mugs to allow the tea to steep. How'd he know I love tea, she thought."

"Okay, enough of that. I'll just go out to your car and put the specs back so we won't forget," when he returned, "so, Evelyn, is it okay if I call you Evelyn,"he asked.

"Please do,"while he was gone, she felt no shame as she snooped around the room, trying to find out as much about him as possible. She wondered about the nice looking woman and the young boy in the photo together with him and didn't know why she even cared who they were.

"You weren't there the last time I came into the showroom. How long have you been there,"he asked, his focus on her made her nervous.

"Well, for most of my adult life I was a nurse. When my husband died, it's barely been a year, I decided I needed a career change,"she spoke softly, watching the fire, enjoying the smell of burning logs, and the flecks of hot sparks, as they spewed unexpectantly from the hearth.

"Well, I'm glad you made the change,"he spoke hesitantly. She smiled, not able to look at him. He circled the rim of his mug with his thumb, hoping she would say something, but she didn't.

The quiet was broken by the ringing of her cell phone. Startled, she jumped to her feet, feeling guilty for having a "moment" with this total stranger. She reached inside her purse for her phone, recognizing the number on the caller ID screen, it was the showroom calling, Paul Senior's personal line. Probably phoning to make sure she didn't botch the job, she pressed the send button,

"Mr. Goldstein, I'm here with Mr. Walker now,"she cleared her throat, thinking he might suspect.. suspect what, that she was having a cup of tea? There's nothing going on, she thought. Yet, she felt guilty for some reason.

"Evelyn? It's Paul Senior,"he spoke loudly, out of breath,

"Okay, I'm just finishing up here and I.."fact was, had he not called she didn't know how long she might have stayed, feeling so comfortable there the way she did.

"Evelyn, I'm not calling about the plans or the meeting. Evelyn, listen to me, I got a call, Evelyn,"he said reluctantly, fumbling and searching for words which failed to come.

"A call," she could barely hear herself speak, so she knew he didn't hear her. She began to shake, knowing this wasn't going to be good, but she couldn't imagine what it could be.

"Yes, you need to go to Cleveland Clinic, dear. Well, it seems your daughter got into a little scuffle with her boyfriend and she's hurt.. Seriously hurt, Evelyn? You there.."

Chapter Fourteen

When she opened her eyes, she didn't recognize the place. It was the smell, the oxygen mask placed over her mouth, and her cold feet, that solved the puzzle. Blake and Paul Senior stood over her, looking gravely concerned.

"Evelyn..Evelyn can you hear me, can you hear me, Evelyn?"Blake repeated softly, "I think she's coming around."He said to Paul. Evelyn could hear a doctor speaking softly with a patient in the next cubicle, somewhere beyond the Care Bear inspired curtains, which divided the two spaces and offered them each privacy. All at once, she remembered, Sissy,

"Sissy!"bolting upright, she tried to get out of bed. The two men attempted to hold her down, but she wouldn't be held down, "ge'et outta my wa'ay, please, I'm begging you. Please, tell me he didn't kill her, please say it, oh God!" A young white, intern ran into the room having heard the scuffling,

"Mrs. Hill, Mrs. Hill, my name is Dr. Briskin, listen to me, calm down, sshh. We need to wait until the results of your x-rays and blood work come back from the lab so we can make sure you're alright, then you can go. I know a lot is happening to you Mrs. Hill, but we have to follow procedure, it won't be much longer. How's your breathing? We've given you some oxygen to help you out.. you passed out Mrs. Hill. Do you remember passing out,"he asked.

"There's nothing wrong with me, I just need to see my daughter, you don't understand, I must get to her, she's in trouble. Am I at Cleveland Clinic hospital, is that where I am," she asked the doctor.

"Yes, you are,"he kept his response brief as he examined her. Pressing down on her stomach first, then he looked into her eyes, asking her to count his fingers, then, he asked her to follow his hand with her eyes. Next, he ordered her to sit up and tested her knee jerk response,

"I just want to make sure you didn't suffer a concussion when you fell, Mrs. Hill," to Blake he asked, "did she hit any sharp objects when she fell?"

"No, I caught her before she actually hit the floor,"Blake answered, shakened, repeatedly pulling on the hairs of his go-tee. A nurse peeked around the curtain and said, "Dr. Briskin, her test results are back now,"

"Be right back,"he said.

Evelyn thought she would lose her mind. She looked uselessly up at the ceiling unable to hold the tears back. Formulating a diabolical plan, she concluded, that if they tried to hold her there any longer, when they all turned their backs, she'd make a dash for it, fight'em if necessary, she spotted some scalpels lying unnoticed on a tray in the corner of the room, she'd cut them if they got in her way. If Sissy were alive, this is where Paul said she would be. Just then, the nurse returned.

"Here let's get you dressed sweety, the tests look good, nothing broken. Your ankle is just badly sprained, we're going to wrap it before you get dressed and I need you to keep it elevated when you get home. Take this wheel chair, one of you can wheel her up to the sixth floor, that's ICU. Her daughter is there.. I have a daughter too, I know this is hard for you. Good luck sweety," Evelyn read the white woman's name tag, Helen Smith, registered nurse. Bless her heart, Evelyn thought."

"Go, Paul, I'm staying," Blake instructed Paul.

"Call me, you must call me. Your daughter has my prayers. Don't come in until you clear it with me, we will cover for you. Take care of your daughter, Evelyn," he kissed her forehead and left quietly.

After having her ankle wrapped, Blake helped her into the wheelchair. The two of them quietly and fearfully made the trip up to the sixth floor. Wheeling her down the long corridor, neither of them spoke. Not up to making small talk, even if she wanted to she was unable to form any words, until she could lay eyes on her daughter.

Finally, reaching the room, she could not believe what she saw. At first glance Sissy seemed completely covered in casts. Her jaw, broken, had been wired. Her left arm and the right leg, both broken, had already been set and placed in casts. Dried blood, lodged underneath the nails of her swollen hands, indicated she'd tried to fight back.

To accommodate the stitches required on her forehead, her bangs were shaved. Evelyn sat in the wheelchair in utter disbelief. She got up from the wheelchair and rested her wilting head on the hospital bed of her daughter, who lie teetering on the edge of death and she cried, loud, gut-wrenching sobs. Her pain, so personal, so private, it had no real language of its' own. Spoken only with grunts, moans, sighs and shrieks, and could only be manufactured by an ordeal of this magnitude. Those were the staples of a language which came from this kind of misery. This pain leveled her lower than the ground, so low, only by looking up, could she see the ground. Still, she needed to say something to her baby. Perhaps hearing the voice of the woman who gave birth to her might motivate her to fight,

"Sissy..baby, it's mommy. I know that you can probably hear me, and I want you to know that I'm here darlin'.. you're not alone. I'm sooo sorry that I didn't do a better job of protecting you. You're so young, nobody this young should be going through something this evil. Mommy is so, so sorry that I didn't know what to do about this. I love you, baby. Please, you must fight, you must get better, please Sissy. I'm so sorryeeee... I'm so sorry, baby!" she cried, holding the limp hand of her child. When she looked up at her daughter, her eyes nearly swollen shut, Evelyn followed the path of Sissy's fresh tears as they fell into the dried tracks of the old tears. She put her arms around Sissy's stomach, put her head to her chest and listened, making sure her heart was still beating. She continued laying her head there and whimpered like a wounded animal. Her daughter almost being killed this way, cut her down to the quick. She'd never felt pain like this before, not even when her man left her suddenly the way he did. What am I to do next? Sit around and wait for him to kill her, she thought, if I don't help her no one will.

"Evelyn," Blake interrupted her thoughts. He'd kept his distance, making sure he gave her enough space to grieve.

"How can I ever thank you," she fell onto his shoulder and sobbed pitifully, cleansing her insides, which had been tainted by this evil thing.

"I checked, they picked'im up already, but it's just a matter of time before he gets out. His bail is set pretty high so, I give'im a couple days and he'll probably be back on the streets. I'll know when he leaves county though, I have somebody looking out for me." he looked at her sympathetically.

"He's going to kill her if I don't do something. Am I the only one who sees that? I'm so scared," she sniffled.

"Working on the police force, I see more of these cases than I care to. Statistics tell us that for African American women, ages fifteen to thirty, homicide resulting from domestic violence, is the number one killer. Did you hear me? I said, the number one killer. Unfortunately, our community is asleep on this one," he said.

"I never knew that," the faceless images of all the dead young women lying in their graves, dying senselessly, spun around inside her head causing her to feel dizzy.

"Does anybody know how Sissy got to the hospital,"she asked him.

"Yea, seems someone by the name of Denise Washington brought her in, you know her,"

"Of course.. Denise. That's her best friend. Do you know where it took place,"she asked. His connections with the police proved invaluable.

"Uh huh, seems the kids all went over to the bowling alley after school for some fun, and that's where it happened, outside in the parking lot,"he reported.

"I see," she tried to imagine Sissy out on Cedar Avenue fighting for her life. Why wasn't I there, she thought.

"Don't do that,"he warned.

"Do what,"

"Blame yourself for this. Leave the blame where it should be, at the feet of the

abuser,"he held her face in his hand.

"Blake I gotta tell ya, I'm a little puzzled and perhaps grossly ignorant when it comes to this kind of thing. Do you know he even threatened to kill her brother if she left him? I had to send my son away, out of the city so I could sleep at night,"

"Tell me a little bit about Brandon, does he go to Sissy's school,"he asked.

"No, he doesn't, but he's always there, checking on her. He rushes over to her school after his building lets out to see who's talking to her, or who she might be talking to. He lives over in Mount Pleasant with his mother and little brother, no father around. Since she began dating him, Sissy talks to no one. She is no longer the same outgoing young-lady I raised. Lately, she's always sad. I just didn't realize kids behaved this way, Blake. When I called the police, the last time he jumped on her, they did nothing, talking about a restraining order. I found out he'd had a bunch of restraining orders, he didn't care about a restraining order, it meant absolutely nothing to him,"she felt better telling someone about it.

"Yea, that's usually the case," he said quietly, summing up the situation.

"I don't like this feeling of helplessness, not being in control of what's going to happen to my daughter. I tried to get her to leave the city, but with only three months remaining before graduation, she insists on graduating with her class..she's the valedictorian of her class. After that, she's outta here. She told me he says he's going to follow her to college. I'm tellin' ya Blake this shit is scary as hell. I fell like a wimp, to have allowed something like this to happen to my daughter. Right now, I have this overwhelming desire to kick his ass, hurt him real bad, so he can see how Sissy feels. Dammit, I want some revenge! I want to see his mother cry some too, wipe that damn smirk off her face, it's certainly her turn to be hurt. I just don't understand why he won't just leave her alone.. why? What makes a man hound a woman this way, it's crazy. I won't sit back and let him kill her. Uh uh, can't do it. Her father would expect more from me than that. Excuse me, but I have to say this, the sorry ass police are waiting until he kills her, I'm sorry I mean no disrespect, but yes they absolutely are.. then and only then will they move and do something. That's when they do their best work, when they have a dead body. But I'll be damned, it ain't going down like that. Me, playing the role of the grieving mother. I can see myself, going. out shopping for another black outfit. The one I wore at my husband's funeral hasn't even collected dust yet and to even be considering burying another one of my loved ones, is mind boggling. For Gods sake, somebody ought to have a little mercy on me, I just buried my husband last year! How much more can I take.. I just can't go out like this! I imagine myself at his trial, walking up to the witness stand, talking about what a wonderful young lady my daughter "was". And then, Brandon's lawyer, getting paid good money, expertly tears down Sissy's character. As he defends Brandon's right to a fair trial, my daughter lies cold in a grave somewhere.. nobody giving a shit about her rights. And you know what Blake, I know you don't know me, and I know I probably appear hysterical to you, but time is running out for me and my child..he's gonna kill her, I can feel it. I gotta find a solution to this nightmare myself, I gotta do it myself, otherwise she won't live to see her next birthday, I can feel it. The handwriting is on the wall. God is showing me.. he's gonna kill her. Damn him..damn him!" she sobbed into his chest.

"Let me know if I can help,"Blake held her tightly. Still hysterical, caught up in her pitiful life, and lost in misery, she did hear him, and thought it was an odd response.

"Ma,"Sissy finally came to. Instantly, when Evelyn looked into her blood shot eyes, she knew her daughter would never be the same.

"Where's Devon, is he alright?"Sissy mouthed the wire that held her jaw in place.. Evelyn didn't call

Devon, she just couldn't deal with his temper knowing that it would inevitably get him into trouble, she could only deal with one child at a time. She deducted from Sissy's question that Brandon had threaten to do something to Devon, again. What's his obsession with Devon, I don't get that, she thought.

"Darlin', how's my baby feelin'? Your brother is fine,"she smiled weakly at her daughter, holding her hand to her mouth, kissing it softly.

"Where's he at? He's not here is he, Ma? Tell Devon not ta come here, please, ma. Brandon is crazy, he tried to kill me..he say he's gon' do it, ma..kill me, cause I'm a no good bitch for going off to college, ma, I don't wanna die..ma?"she fell back into her fitful sleep. Evelyn hung her head low, her burden so heavy, forced it down.

She couldn't be sure just when the idea struck her, hitting her on the head like a ton of bricks, but like all other ideas in various stages of infant development, she cuddled it in her arms, loving the feelings of relief it gave her. Having feelings for it, the same as a nurturing mother of new born pups, allowing it to suckle her sustenance, never growing weary of the constant pulling and tugging on her body as she lie there, learning to incorporate the intrusion to her body, as a much anticipated part life.

Like all other ideas, it slowly seeped into her psyche, beginning from a subliminal suggestion, little by little, snowballing, taking over, as if it should have always been there. It became as familiar to her as old cousin Harriet, whose house everyone loved to visit, because she always had good food, and made good company too.

This idea of killing, Brandon specifically, came to her as an instant revelation, falling down from the sky, reaching out especially for her, because only she possessed the fertile ground it needed in which to thrive. Once the idea took up residence in her mind, it calmed her, like a tranquilizer, providing a zombie like calm she desperately needed.

"I will have to get rid of him, permanently. Yes.. that is the answer. His death will mean life for Sissy," she thought peacefully. She had no illusions that killing him would solve all of her problems, in fact, she admitted to herself, new problems would evolve as a result of her decision. She winced, when she pictured herself wearing the orange suit, chained to strangers, walking to a dingy cell which she'd call home for life. Even with the images of such a dismal picture, she still smiled, when she pictured her baby, later in life, with babies of her own, holding them, smiling at them, playing with them. No, he would not take that from her.

For the first time in months, she saw things clearly, as if blinders had been lifted from her eyes. She'd been left with no options. Simply put, in order for Sissy to live, Brandon had to die. That would make her a murderer. She would simply have to learn to live with that, he had forced her to go there. "When I get home, I'll get the number out of the drawer that Juney gave me and I'll make the arrangements," she thought calmly.

"Mrs. Hill? How's she doin'," Denise returned to the hospital after going home to get her mother's car. She imagined Betty on the phone, calling everybody she knew, running her mouth, tearing Sissy down. Of course in Betty's mind, the gossip would be well intentioned, because at the end of the conversation, she'd tell everybody to pray for Sissy, which absolved her of any guilt.

Tonight, Evelyn didn't care, she couldn't think about Betty right now, she needed to try and save her daughter's life.

"Well, sweety she's holding on, just pray for her. Thank you so much. What would we do without you, Neicey," Evelyn hugged her.

"She's my buddy, my gurl, my road dawg. She has to get better. Mrs. Hill I'm so scared,"Denise broke down. Evelyn held her until she calmed down.

"Me to Neicey, but together, we will get through this,"

"She had no business wit' him, but she was scared, I understand that now. I didn't understand that before,"Denise dried her tears with a hanky offered to her by Blake. He seemed to be all over the place, helping. Evelyn studied him carefully for a minute.

"Neicey?"Sissy's words sounded garbled.

"Haay, you woke? Don't try ta talk, let me do all the talking." Denise went to Sissy's bed and began to catch her up on their friends. From time to time Sissy gave a weak smile, often drifting in and out of sleep.

"Denise, I'm going to go and look at Sissy's chart and then go home to shower and grab some Pjs, how long will you be here," Evelyn asked.

"As long as you need me to be, I won't leave her,"

"There's a security guard sitting right by the nurses station, see..right there, he's going to keep a look out also while I'm gone, okay,"she kissed Neicey on the forehead.

"On it," Denise said flipping through the television channels, searching for hip hop videos.

Once she checked Sissy's chart and felt satisfied that medically Sissy would pull through, Evelyn said to Blake,

"I seem to be imposing on you again and again. I need to go home, get a shower and a car to drive, you mind,"

"I'm not going to leave you, I will take you home and then come back for you. While you're showering it will give me a chance to wrap up some business. I'm prepared to sit this one out," he said guardedly, not sure how she felt about him including himself.

It was strange. She didn't really know him, but she couldn't bring herself to object. She noticed him stepping right into her life, doing the things Lamont would do, such as being there, checking on things, making inquiries and driving her home. Those were the things her man had always done for her and their children. She wondered too about the sorrow which this familiar stranger exuded. She saw it, a shadow that constantly followed him around, she heard it whispering, and now she felt it, attempting to equally divide its' gloom between them.

"Okay, let's go." Too tired to think of doing things any other way, she prayed it would all work out.

Chapter Fifteen

Evelyn, in a rush, quickly slid her key into the lock, impatient pushed it a couple of times before she heard the familiar click pulling the bolt lock over, opening the door. The house remained quiet and tranquil, only the hum of the refrigerator could be heard, everything was just as she'd left it. It was ironic, she thought, this morning heading for her peaceful work environment, enjoying the commute, every now and then laughing at Tom Joyner or Sybil, to then return this evening to a life turned topsy turvy. If she didn't know any better she thought she'd been punk'd, or perhaps unknowingly a candid camera contestant. She half expected to be accosted by a celebrity host, bent over in hysterical laughter pointing to a hidden camera.

Exhausted, she tossed her keys onto the granite table top in the kitchen, kicked off her Manolo Blahniks black t-strap pumps, opened the stainless steel fridge and reached inside for a bottle of Aquafina to refresh her parched mouth. Blake said he would return within the hour, giving her just enough time to shower, throw some clothes into her gym bag and make the call. Sipping on the bottled water, she looked around her stylishly decorated home and thought about how meaningless it all was compared to the feelings she had towards her family.

Her mother's plump, round face came into focus, grief stricken, from the possibility of one day, outfitted in generic orange jumpsuits, prison chains and butch like appearance. Her mother might not survive such a scene. Still, she thought it futile to share any segment of this information with anyone. Not even telling Lisa about Sissy's abuse, the way she saw it, it was implausible that anyone she knew could solve the problem, so what would be the point in blabbing the embarrassing details of such a humiliating experience. Really.. when giving it thorough consideration, why did they need to know? She needed answers and solutions, not feigned sympathy that amounted to no more than the assembling of information to pass on to the haters. Plus, she believed that drama of a sensitive nature, involving her children, should always be kept private, too intimate to share. If Lamont were here, she knew what he would say, this is family business, it's not information for you to go out and loosely toss around out in the streets. Besides, your so- called peeps, not able to help themselves, had this nagging habit of blaming the victim. Predictably she expected to hear the whispers, behind her back of course, coming from the well intentioned, saying deviously, well, what she doin' wit somebody like that anyway, or, what did she do ta bring that on herself.

Stepping out of the shower, she toweled dried her long curly hair and decided, in order to save time, she'd leave it naturally curly, instead of blow- drying it straight. She pulled on some sweats and packed enough clothes for three days. Grabbing her cell phone, she forward her land-line calls to her cell phone. That way if Devon called, he wouldn't know what was going on.

Easing her night- stand drawer open, half expecting to find the devil crouched lethally inside, she studied the card suspiciously, never picking it up. It looked out of place amongst the hair-pins, head scarf, old family photos, toe-nail clippers and her bible. In its' foreign surroundings, the card lay awkwardly atop the contents of the drawer, as if anticipating her return.

Staring out the window at the falling snow, as if somewhere between the flakes she'd find a way out. She knew that if she were ever going to turn back, it would have to be now. Instead, with shaking hands, as her beating heart pounded heavily against her chest, she picked up the phone and pressed the corresponding numbers. Looking around the room, she double-checked, making sure nobody could hear the conversation. Feeling the conviction of her actions, already she'd begun acting guilty. The phone began ringing. She held her breath. On the fourth ring, just as she was about to hang up, chicken out,

"Hello?" The deep voice answered. Terrified, as if bitten unexpectantly by a snake, she threw the phone clear across the room. Standing in the corner as if cornered by the snake, looking down at the phone, afraid to touch it, because, she recognized the voice. It was the voice of, Blake Walker, he was, "Mighty."

For some ten minutes, she remained stooped over in the corner of her bedroom, like a trapped animal afraid that moving would end its' life, staring at the phone, an inanimate object that bought unfathomable perplexity into her formerly simple life. Not knowing what else to do, she grabbed her things and headed for the only car available, Sissy's Corolla. Jumping into the car, she headed straight for his house. "What the hell is going on?" she thought, speeding down Chagrin Boulevard.

He sat waiting outside, in the cold, looking small and insignificant next to the huge pillars of the Georgian traditional.

"What are you drinking," was all he said, when he opened her car door. The quiet and stillness of the winter night, provided a suitable back drop for the dark revelation, "come inside and you decide what you want. If I don't have what you want, I'll go out and get it," they stood facing each other in a merciful stand-off, neither knowing in what direction to take the conversation.

Inside, he mixed her a scotch and water, neat. She swallowed the icy warm liquid, closing her eyes as it slid down, rapidly melting the ice which clung to her insides. She needed to think for a minute before she spoke. She finished off her drink and handed the empty glass back to him for a refill,

"Why,"she said softly. Without turning around from the bar he answered,

"The other room in there.. the one Goldstein and Goldstein just finished decorating, it belonged to my dead son. He's been dead now, for three years. I'd been keeping it as sort of a shrine, you know, feeling close to him every time I went in there. Suddenly, one day, sitting amongst his things, clinging to the past, it clicked inside my head that it was time I moved on, at least physically. To do that you gotta get rid of the stuff, otherwise without wanting to, you'll keep going back to it..not healthy."

Her instinct had been right on the money, it was the pain she'd felt coming from him at the hospital. She walked over to him and turned him around, forcing him to look at her,

"I'm so very, very sorry. How did it happen..can you talk about it,"she asked, taking her drink from him as she guided him back to the sofa,

"He was beaten to death by gang members. They'd been after him to become a part of the group. You're going to find this hard to believe but they needed a form of transportation, and they just decided that my son, Kareem, that was his name, should just turn his car over to them, it seemed logical to them." He got up, went to the armoire and pulled out photos of Kareem. Evelyn stared at the handsome young man, who looked so much like Blake and grieved for such senseless loss of young life.

"Are you married,"she asked timidly.

"Was..the marriage died with my son. We didn't have anything else in common,"he shook his head, thinking about his past life.

"Tell me, what happened," she asked, handing the picture back to him.

"Well," he sighed, "it was a simple case of me downplaying what my son told me. He told me and his mother that there were problems with some guys who hung around the school I didn't and he didn't understand that they were actually a gang. See, he didn't attend school in our neighborhood. My son aspired to become the next Winton Marsalis, he was a magnificent trumpet and saxophone player. He lived and breathed his music and he begged us to let him go to a school in the inner city that focused on the talents and gifts students had. So, anxious to see him excel in his music, we allowed him to go to this school, school of music, you know it," Evelyn nodded her head, "and, these particular gang members didn't even attend school. But they're looking at Kareem driving into the city everyday in his nice ride, and they decide they're going to get him as part of the gang..simple, this way they don't have to worry about transportation anymore, cause they dabbled in petty theft and other crimes, so you can see why they'd need a car. Turns out it wasn't quite as simple as they thought it would be, Kareem refused and.. they got hot. Next thing I know, they get totally pist, not being able to control Kareem and things get violent.. they were just going to force him to become a member. So.. he continues to refuse and then things get nasty, they start.. scratching up his car, taking his stuff. I did everything, I talked to the cats, I went up to the school..I stopped in during the day, I was always there..you know, making my presence felt. Then, for a minute everything was quiet, it seemed as if they'd moved on. We got relaxed, stop looking out and then, one day, I saw him off to school that morning.. it was the one day I didn't go over there.. and he never made it home, they shot him in the school parking lot, took his car and his saxophone. I didn't believe it when they told me my son was dead. Sometimes, I still look for him to come through that door ," he finished sadly.

"Blake,"she said.

"Yea," his voice breaking up.

"What's it like.. how bad is it..loosing a child I mean,"she asked carefully.

"Well, let me just put it this way, I will never, ever heal. The pain is constant, on going, relentless, ever present and cruel. My chest is sore from the constant pain in my heart. I often wish I were dead because I'm so tired of living with the pain, but because I am not dead, I simply go through the motions of living. I am what some would call, the walking dead. And that, my friend is why I will do whatever I have to, to make sure you never feel pain like that,"his tears fell silently. Silent tears are the worst, opening the closed soffet, dripping annoyingly, at times rushing forward unwanted, telling the whole world that inexplicable pain exists deep within your soul.

"So..is that how you got involved..I mean are you involved,"she asked guardedly.

"The answer is yes. It is a well guarded piece of information in our community. I can't say very much about it, only that I help women..just like yourself. Women, alone, who's lives, or the lives of their children are at risk. Usually, it's just a matter of arranging for the abuser to be roughed up, if that ends the abuse, then my work is done, but if I'm dealing with a persisitent abuser, one who isn't going to move on just cause you gave'im a good ass whuppin', then, I gotta take it to another level. Understand one thing Evelyn, I never, ever shed innocent blood, it has to be a life and death situation for the victim. I will often assist a family in using what's available to them legally, which ain't much. As a detective with the police department, I know first hand, the limitations of the law. Make no mistake Evelyn, if you leave this problem unresolved, he will kill her. It's a cold hard fact and that's how you gotta deal with it, cold and hard. But you're not alone, I'm here for you," he said.

"This all feels so weird, I mean, at first I can't know you at all, and now, I know almost everything about you. Practically speaking, I should fear you, but I don't. In fact I feel that I have more in common with you right now, than any other person in this world. You are the only person who can relate to the fear I'm living with. Is your job in jeopardy,"she asked.

"I'm not worried,"

"I feel badly for what I'm asking you to do, it's wrong..my momma never prepared me for nothing like this," she looked into his eyes.

"You know Evelyn, one of these days, these cats are going to realize that, knocking women around may just bring down retaliation on them they never dreamed of, somebody has to put some fear in dey asses and that's what I'm about, putting some fear into these cats, where none existed. If I gotta take a couple of them out, then so be it, our women are dying Evelyn, nobody seems to care,"He paused, looking at her questioningly,

"Now, my question to you Evelyn, is, can I trust you,"he searched her eyes imploringly, pulling her close to him, their spirits merged by a need to kick injustice in the ass.

"Yes.. you can."she answered, allowing him to seal the deal with a kiss.

Chapter Sixteen

Detective Smith closed the file cabinet, lost in thought, he slowly walked back to his desk, not watching where he was going, as he transformed himself back to the scene of the crime. Eyes glued to the report, he bumped into the ledge in the doorway, hitting his head hard, "dammit, that hurt," he thought, rubbing the beginnings of a small lump.

Returning his attention to the report, he studied the information intensely for what felt like the hundredth time. It seemed a routine report, same information, where, when, who, time of death etc. Uniquely, his keen nose sniffed out the development of a pattern.

Three homicides happening within twenty-three months of each other. In each case, one bullet to the head, nice and clean. The use of a silencer in a crowded environment, guaranteed annonimity, or at least, bought the killer a chunk of time before anybody realized someone had been hit. Each homicide occurred at events with, wall to wall people, one at a high school football game, the other at a parade and another at a community picnic.

He studied the photo from the morgue of the latest victim, eyes permanently shut down to life, lying stiff and lifeless on the cold steel slab. According to the report, he had been approximately six feet tall, one hundred and eighty pounds, dark complexion black kid, nineteen- years old. A good-looking kid, however, the residuals of a hard street life hung spookily over his frame, especially the face.

"What happened to you partner? Were you makin' an ass of yourself? Speak to me, give me something here," he asked mainly of himself. His phone rang.

"Detective Smith?" he answered, still looking at the photo.

"Dad," it was his daughter, Becky.

"Sweetheart.. How are ya?" he asked, happy to hear from her. When he and Becky's Mom divorced some five years ago, he'd been afraid that the damage to her might have been irreparable. Going through a teenage rebellion phase, complete with the drugs and alcohol, staying out late, he felt responsible, the divorce had shaken up her world. Then, just as suddenly as the demon appeared, it just as quickly disappeared.

Becky managed to complete three years at the university even though she married, in his opinion, an idiot. The best thing that came out of the joke of a marriage, was his grandson, Johnny. When Johnny, the love of his life, turned two years old, he purchased a small sailboat, for the two of them, spending many happy afternoons together, down on the lake, fishing or just hanging out.

"I'm fine Dad. Anything interesting come along today?" she asked.

"Yeah, I might run it by you tonight. Are we still having spaghetti at your place tonight?" he asked, hoping she wasn't calling to cancel. He didn't relish the idea of eating alone, again. He didn't date much, he found it awkward and expensive and more times than not, the company sucked. Most evenings were spent alone, eating TV dinners by the television, later falling asleep with a good book.

"Yes, that's what I'm calling about. But Dad, I was wondering if you could pick Johnny up from school on your way over? When I get out of school I'd like to come straight home and start dinner, have it ready when you get here," she finished.

How come Josh can't pick him up, he wanted to question her, but didn't. His son in law, was a sore subject, one he avoided. A sorry excuse for a husband, with no ambition, he couldn't even hold down a job. He knew the best thing for him to do was, to keep his mouth shut and wait it out, positive the marriage wouldn't last.

"Of course honey. Can I pick up anything else? I don't mind," He said kindly.

"No, that's it Dad, thanks. See you tonight." She seemed relieved.

He hung up the phone and returned his thoughts to the young man in the photo. What he really needed to do was to run his thoughts by somebody else, get another opinion about the possible connection between the three homicides.

He looked up from his desk and realized that most people had already begun leaving for lunch. It was Friday, payday, everybody would be over at Sol's on fourteenth-street, where they served up the best corned-beef he ever tasted. He closed out his computer, grabbed his jacket and the file, he would put back on his way out.

Outside, he cringed, looking at the dreary, gray, overcast sky of October. The menagerie of fall colors competed miserably, doing little to brighten up the depressing picture. As he made the walk over to Sol's, his thoughts, again, returned to the photo of the homicide victim. He remembered his name.. Brandon Jones. He couldn't be sure but, he thought he might've heard that name somewhere before. He'd asked around. He kept seeing his face in his mind. Morgue photos often haunted him that way.

Feeling the beginnings of a light shower, falling onto his nose, he pulled his jacket to and buttoned it. Turning onto fourteenth street, from the corner he could see that Sol's was packed with standing room only.

Inside Sol's, the music of Motown, lifted his spirits, moving his head to the music of the Temptations, he scanned the room to see whose booth he could squeeze into.

Oh, there's Carl over there, ump.. but I don't want to sit with Darby. Not after that last time he got drunk and called me an asshole. Naw.. Let's see..they're really no tables available. It is really crowded in here, I don't understand why they don't expand the place, they got the customers, he looked around. Maybe he could ease into a booth just as someone got up. He'd have to watch carefully. Placing his order with the waitress, he paid his tab, and took his beer with him as he looked for a seat. As luck would have it, he saw one of his co-workers, Blake Walker sitting with Mike Bernstein and Mike was leaving. Smith rushed over, uninvited,

"My man, Blake hi ya been?" he smiled as he sat down without asking.

"Harry, man, you got it. How da hell you been? You still digging around in grave yards for evidence, man? I hollered when Mike told me about that," Blake laughed.

"Well, you know, anything for my public." Smith teased running his hands through his thinning blonde hair.

"Yeah, right. So, what's up with you, man? How's that cute grandson of yours?" Blake asked as he finished his corned beef sandwich, taking a swig from his beer to wash it down.

"Man, he's growing in leaps and bounds. He is the smartest kid ever. I take him fishing with me all the time. He already knows how to bait the hook and what kind of bait to use. I'm going over there for dinner tonight. He is some kind of special, that kid is," he finished, picturing Johnny in his mind.

"I know, man." Blake said sadly, looking out the window, at nothing in particular. Smith wanted to bit his tongue off rambling on about Johnny that way. He knew that Blake had lost his only child, about three years ago. The entire precinct attended the funeral services and all had been brought to tears listening to the taped rendition of Blake's son's rendition of Precious Lord. Smith would never forget the unusual style and the passion with which he played. The young man had talent beyond belief and Blake had been so proud of him.

"Listen man, I been looking into something over at the station, you know snooping around like I always do, and I'd like to run something by you," he leaned forward. He didn't want everybody to hear. He'd had co-workers take credit for his hard work before, it wasn't going down like that again. He trusted Blake.

"What's up?" Blake said.

"Well, I think I see a connection between at least three homicides laying cold over there," He began.

"Homicides? Which ones? Have they already been dumped into cold case," Blake asked, not really interested, having recently been promoted to identity theft.

"Yep. I've been focusing on the last one. A youngster by the name of, Brandon Jones. You heard of him before, or about the case?" Smith ended. Suddenly Blake choked on the beer as he swallowed. Choking and coughing, his beer mixed with spit, spewed out from Blakes mouth and landed on Smith's face. Blake jumped up, embarrassed, and began dabbing at Smith's face and clothes, with his soiled napkin,

"Awh shit! Look at the mess I made, man. I swallowed my beer too fast, you know how that is. I am so sorry," Blake rambled.

" It's okay, it's okay man. A little spit, even yours never hurt anybody." Smith laughed, motioning for Blake to sit back down.

Blake remained standing.

"Listen, man, sorry, I hadn't heard about that one. Run it by me another time, I'm being paged.

"Oh? I didn't hear your pager." Smith said, just like the detective that he was.

"Naw, you see.. I got it on vibrate. There's something I need to take care of. I'm gonna push on up outta here. Look there's Ron and David, run it by them. They'll keep you company. Give me a rain check, okay?" Blake finished hurriedly. He waved to David and Ron to come over. Blake threw his jacket over one shoulder and was out the door before he could get the other arm securely inside the jacket, leaving behind him a cloud of suspicion, that was not lost on Smith.

Chapter Seventeen

Harry knocked on Louis O'Neal's door. The task ahead saddened him beyond words. Nothing could be worst than having to bust another officer. What made it even worse, he and Blake liked each other, had often been there for one another, covering each other's tail. He knew that if he didn't come forward with the information, eventually someone else would. Worse case scenario, could be the media getting their grubby, manipulative hands on the information, putting their evil spin on it. Reporting the existence of the blue wall, causing heightened public distrust, making it even harder for them than it already is, to work successfully within the community.

This one time he wished he hadn't been so persistent. But the last killing, which took place at the high school football game, rekindled his curiosity about this pattern he sensed developing. Again, the victim was shot between the eyes, using the same type of weapon. Again, the shooting took place during a crowded event, nobody saw or heard anything.

Coincidentally, each time, Walker showed up immediately after the shooting, supposedly, moonlighting as an off duty officer. At first it was a small detail that grated on his nerves, driving him to investigate further. With the kind of money Walker had, Smith knew for sure he couldn't be taking these penny- anny security jobs because he needed the money, so why was he there? It was an excellent cover. Harry checked, and discovered that Walker was present at the last two shootings as well. He secretly decided not to look any further.

The victim, Brandon Jones, died in the lap of his girlfriend at a football game from a single gun shot to the head, just like the others. The young lady, Serrita Hill, the school's academic star, headed to one of the most prestigious, southern colleges in the states on a full scholarship, yet she couldn't even leave her house unless this guy Brandon, allowed her to.

While checking other unrelated details, in another case, Harry stumbled upon the connection between this young lady and his co-worker, Walker. Sadly, he learned that Walker had been sleeping with the girl's mother, he loved her. He empathized with Walker's reasoning, and as wrong as it was, there was a part of him, the father part, that secretly said, right on.

The victim, a professional street thug, with a long history of abusing women, had recently been picked up and booked for beating the girl so severely, she was hospitalized. Harry thought about Becky and how much he loved her. If he found her in a violent, life-threatening relationship like this one, with no options available, he wondered, would he sit idly by and wait until she was killed to act, or would he take matters into his own hands. He knew the answer without giving it a thought. He wouldn't allow anybody to take his daughter out like that. His heart went out to both Mrs. Hill and Walker. They probably saved the young girl's life. But you don't take a life to give a life, at least that's what he'd been taught, and it sounded right to him.

Walker committed a crime and he must be held accountable for his actions. He'd been careful, and putting a case together against him would take work and for Harry there were no usual feelings of jubilation when a mystery had been solved. When good citizens are aided or assisted by criminal activity, then society runs the risk of others following the example, an out of control situation. People committing random acts of vigilante heroism, he just wasn't comfortable with that, turning his head, looking the other way, which is what a lot of his coworkers would expect of him.

Harry knocked on the door of Lou's office again, harder this time,

"Come in." Lou yelled, as he finished up a phone conversation.

Harry nervously tried opening the door. Fumbling, his slippery hands were unable to grip the doorknob because his palms had grown sweaty and clammy, anxiety gripping him like the death grip of bolder contrictor, squeezing the very breath out of him in nervous anticipation of this moment. Lou shook his bald head impatiently when finally, Harry literally stumbled into his office. Harry couldn't be sure how his coworkers would react to the revelation. If he were honest, his forecast was, the term snitch would be coined when referring to him from this day forward.

"Okay, but you can't manufacture evidence, Bill.. you either have it or you don't." Lou spoke curtly into the phone, which he held with his right shoulder, rolling his big green eyes to the sky contemptuously.

Harry took a seat amongst all the clutter. Empty soda cans were strewn about on the old desk which was covered in old food stains, evidence of the many working lunches Lou had held. Harry sat behind the unattended papers stacked so high, you could hardly see Lou's face while sitting across from him. The odor of stale cigarettes and rotting food permeated the room, making Smith feel a little queezy.

An uncharacteristically warm day in November, the antique fan on Lou's desk turned weakly from side to side, in a failed attempt to cool the room and force the odor elsewhere.

"That's my final decision..well, talk to Myers maybe he can help. Okay, gotta go, I got somebody waiting to talk to me..uh huh..yep, good by." Lou finished, then said to him,

"What'cha got for me?"

"I need to run some things by you, Lou. Is now a good time," Harry asked.

"No, but later won't be any better..shoot," Lou said as he shuffled papers around, distracted by all of the correspondence that lay unattended to on his desk. Harry sat back in his seat; thinking that what he had to say would sound better that way. Straightening his tie as if it were tied too tightly around his neck, he said pointedly,

"I'm here about the Jones' case. The third unsolved homicide in the last twenty- three months. The victim was shot in the head at the high school football game.. about a month ago?" he said trying to get Lou's attention.

Lou continued to look down at the document he had in his hand, but nodded his head in recognition of Harry's presence. Still, he wasn't listening to him.

"Well, I'm ready to put a case together.. against Walker," Harry finished, sure that would get his attention, undivided.

Lou's head jerked upright, his eyes narrowed in disbelief.

"What Walker you talkin' about? Not one of my top detectives, not that Walker," Lou asked suspiciously, looking at Harry incredulously. Harry lowered his gaze and said,

"I'm afraid so. I've had him under surveillance for a while, most of which I did myself, on my own time and everything leads straight back to him. He takes these security jobs to place himself at the scene and to have a reason for being there. In each case he was the one that called for help, yet, never saw a thing. I have one faint print from the booth where the killer took the shot from. I'm waiting for the answer but I'm pretty sure it's his. I checked, nobody uses the booth because it needed repair. Instead of repairing it, the school district built a brand new one. I also found shoe prints, fresh ones and I need a warrant to see if the shoes can be traced to Walker." Harry said finally, glad to get it all out.

Lou's mouth hung open as Harry recanted his theory. A little bead of dribble began to form at the corner of Lou's mouth, threatening to fall as a result of his laborious concentration. Slowly, a look of disbelief crept up his neck, painstakingly washing over his entire face.

"You've finally lost it, haven't ya? Ya just waltz in here and calmly announce that one of my best detectives, doubles as a hit man. Ya may have some prints here and a few there, but when it comes down to an accusation as serious as this, ya need proof, proof enough to build an entire case on, and if Walker is involved he wouldn't be so stupid as to just map things out for ya! That man has too much knowledge to just hand himself over to ya like that. Go on, get outta here, you've gone too far this time!" Lou yelled as he shooed Harry away like a persistent fly.

Harry knew that if he didn't prove what he was saying was in fact the truth, then Lou would always think of him as some kind of an ignorant-head. Harry calmed himself down and spoke slowly,

"Now, Lou I know that you know, somehow Walker is involved. But what you really want from me, is for me to ignore what I've learned about his involvement. And don't worry, I have not spoken about this matter with anyone other than you, and I never will. But what you and many others in this department will want to do is a sweep. I simply cannot do that , believe me I thought about it, but I just can't. There's a problem with you and I and the others just looking the other way, because Blake happens to be one of us. Are we any better than those people in the community who look the other way when a crime is committed, because it's one of their loved ones or somebody they know and respect? We can't just have people, any people going around deciding for themselves what should be done about the Brandon Jones' of this world. Granted he was evil. Admit it, we both have locked up a lot of devils in our time, surprisingly some manage to pull their lives together later on in life. So, who are we to make that call," Smith said, finally.

"If I thought for one second that what you are talking about had even an ounce of truth to it, I would be happy to listen to your fanatical rambling's on, but since I don't, I have but one thing to say to you Smith.. bu-bye. Go on, get outta here, I got people ta see and eggs ta fry, go on, git outta here." Lou waved Smith away a second time. Smith knew that if he didn't make Lou believe him, from this day forward, he would think of Smith as an idiot of the worse kind, the kind who rats on a friend.

His mother taught him that in any loud argument, if you really want to be heard, speak softly and save your best blow for last. So, he pulled out all the stops as he headed for the door. Holding the knob in his hand he said, barely audible,

"Walker is banging the girl's mother," he breathed heavily. Lou gasped and groaned,

"Close the door."

Chapter Eighteen

Tower City was an unusual mixture of the old and the new Cleveland. Cleverly, history and futuristic architecture had been blended together to make for an exciting shopping experience. Beneath the high ceilings, lay the city's tracks, connecting the east and west side to the downtown area, which encompassed the Rock 'n Roll Hall of Fame and the increasingly popular, Cleveland Flats' area.

Even though Christmas was over, and New Years only hours away, shoppers continued to pound the pavement in relentless pursuit of bargains. Over by the escalators, a trio ensemble played beautiful Christmas music and Blake decided to take a seat and listen while he waited for Evelyn. They would sneak away to the old Stouffer restaurant, find a secluded booth, and have a quiet dinner together. When she walked by him, after allowing some time to pass, he would follow. Averting any chance of being seen together in such a public place as this. Blake didn't want to make it easy for anyone to make the connection between the two of them. They still needed to lay low for a minute.

Blake picked up an abandoned newspaper and began to scan the entertainment section. After dinner he wanted to take her someplace special. His favorite jazz club, according to the paper, would be serving up some raw jams tonight. A good friend of his, Jason, owned the club and he'd designed it with private little alcoves upstairs, with separate entrances, from which they could still see the set. He'd phone ahead, and reserve one for him and Evelyn. Scaning the movie section, as usual, he didn't see anything mentally stimulating. He turned the page to see what was happening at the playhouse.

Slightly lifting the paper to clear his lap, he noticed a pair of old, black, Stacey Adams' shoes, standing directly in front of him. Thinking that odd, Blake slowly lowered the newspaper to see who the shoes belonged to. He was startled to see his coworker, Detective Smith, standing there, staring blankly at the back of the paper. His behavior, was disquieting to say the least, but then that accurately described his entire demeanor. Smith's hair, ruffled and unkept, typified his comportment. The old gray blazer that he wore everyday with its' worn, frayed, spots on the collar and the matching gray trousers having long since lost the crease they had, when purchased new, was Smith's distinguishing presentation.

A sense of foreboding slowly slithered up Blake's ankle, snaking its way on up to his knees. Passing through his groin area, where it plunged heavily into the bottom of his rectum, reeling him into the urge to defecate. Oily beads of sweat glistened at his front hairline, decoding the secret, diabolical plan of life and death he'd perpetrated.

The little trio began playing Silent Night as shoppers and on lookers paused, some gathered around the trio reflecting on the personal sentimentality of the song. Blake too, remembered the excitement he'd felt as a child when he heard that song. To him it meant all things good and pure, like the group of carolers pictured on Christmas cards in their nice white robes. And of the family home all decorated in red and white, flashed inside his head, carressing all the pleasure centers in his brain. The image, freeze framed, was of his Daddy, hauling in the biggest tree he could find, placing it smack dab in the middle of the living room, so no matter where you went in the house, you had to pass or see the Christmas tree. His mother filling the house with the aroma of freshly baked cakes, pies, rolls, and cookies. He and his brother Earl, their mouths watering, trying to figure out, where their feast should begin, had to constantly be warned my mama not to act like little pigs. Those were happy times, but they couldn't compare with what he felt since meeting Evelyn. He found himself dreaming of how it would have been, had they met under different circumstances.

It would've been perfect, he thought. Perfection however was not a part of life. Even his love for her had not made everything perfect, but it had made life worth living.

He thought about her. She was the core of his existence. Whenever he'd loved, which hadn't happened often, he loved hard, intensely, obsessively. He pictured her in his kitchen, lovingly preparing a meal for them, as she so often did, making sure everything was just so. He remembered how he'd sat at the table watching her, from behind, fixing dinner, as he dreamt of the nasty things he'd do later to that perfectly rounded behind of hers. She'd turned around, and caught him looking at her that way,

"You.. dog.. you." She teased. He'd barked in agreement and continued on in his dream. She knew his every thought, his moods, desires, regrets and dreams.

Later that night as he covered her naked body, he deliberately lingered at her swollen breasts, holding them, sucking them, while wondering about the possibility of new life. Through love glazed eyes, he looked down at her as she lie there, held tightly in his arms, her caramel skin, so velvety and edible. Falling under the spell of her big, beautiful, brown eyes that pleaded with him to make the world right again. Her crinkled hair lay fanned out on the pillow and he'd buried his face in it, drinking in her scent, lost in the dream he'd had at the table.

Afterwards, he thought about the second heartbeat that might lay buried deep inside her womanhood. He dared not ask. Things were already tough enough. He knew he was complicating things even more, but he'd lost all sense of reasoning as a result of loving her. She made him crazy, careless, stupid and selfish. She'd reconnected the light in his life, lovingly bringing him in out of the dark, putting the spark back into his once dead eyes. He had to have her, all of her and subconsciously he admitted, that he wanted her pregnant.

Now Smith was standing there obtrusively, in front of him, threatening everything that was good and sweet in his life. His timing sucked.

"Meeting somebody?" Smith asked suspiciously, searching Blake's face for answers.

"Just chillin', man. What are you doing here?" Blake struggled to sound normal.

"Walker, I came to talk to you, man. I just left your house...I'm sorry, man, it's all over, I know everything. I knew from your phone conversation you were meeting her here. I had your phone tapped. I've been listening to your conversations." Smith finished.

"With friends like you, who the hell needs enemies," Walker said sarcastically.

"Walker you know friendship has nothing to do with this, we're talking alleged murder here,"

"Right..key word is, alleged, remember that."Blake said, bitterly.

Even though Smith was standing, his shoulders were slumped way over. A wave of sadness hung over Smith, following him around like a shadow, engulfing Blake, making him feel as though he were drowning.

From a distance Blake could see Evelyn walking down the busy sidewalks, moving from side to side to maneuvering her way through the crowd of people. Slowly looking from left to right, closely inspecting the holiday displays or whatever caught her fancy, unaware that trouble was only a few feet away. Wearing the fur coat he'd given her for Christmas, wearing it elegantly as only she could, she stopped and stood in front of the record store, studying the 57 chevy displayed in the window, sitting on a pedestal which turned it around and around in a circle, very slowly. When she walked away she noticed him sitting there. She could feel that he knew she was there even though her view of him was blocked by Smith.

Blake feared Smith would turn around and see her there. He never let his eyes stray from Smith's. What seemed like hours were only seconds as he fought desperately to concentrate on Smith. His mind scrambled to think of what he would do if Smith saw her.

The music continued to play on as his fear of her discovery mounted. He hoped she wouldn't come any closer, willing her to stop in his mind. Smith's back still faced her as he waited for Blake's response. She began walking towards them. His heart beat faster and faster from fear. She continued on towards him with a beautiful smile, spread widely across her face. He coughed, almost choking on the lump stuck in his throat that hindered his swallowing. He fought the urge to yell out to her. Instead, he kept his eyes fixed on Smith. Abruptly, intuition caused her to stop, dead in her tracks. Like a beautiful Siamese cat, who sensed trouble, she paused, in mid air. She gave careful consideration of Smith standing there talking to Blake. Analyzing the situation intently, slowing down , sorting out the scene in her mind. Gradually, she turned, picked up her pace, and hurried towards the restaurant, the fur coat flailing behind her.

He remembered how he'd made love to her in that fur coat in front of a warm fire, and how afterwards she'd become hysterical, telling him about this feeling she had. She predicted that this day would come and he hadn't heeded her warnings.

"Her? Who exactly are you talking about?" Blake responded unconvincingly. The entire encounter, draining him.

Smith shuffled his feet and looked away, embarrassed by the cat and mouse game he was playing with a fellow comrade, he highly respected.

"I know everything, Walker. I've been to your house..I found the shoes that match the prints from the announcement booth at the high school where the Jones shooting took place. I can place you there. I calculated the footage, and I know that is where the shot came from. I don't have the gun yet and other parts of the case I'm not prepared to discuss with you at this time. You two willing to come in without an arrest warrant or do I have to put your business on front street? Nobody else knows about this," Smith said sympathetically.

Blake could tell that after all his hard work, and he knew Smith had worked hard to bring him in, the pay off wasn't what Smith had anticipated, it left him feeling short changed.

"She's not involved in this, Smith. I'm going down alone, man, or not at all." Blake said angrily.

I've blown it, I'm acting as if I know who she is, he thought erratically.

Smith was not moved. It only fueled his determination.

"I'm sorry but I...." Smith began. Blake interrupted him.

Blake got up and pulled Smith over to the isolated corridor that led to the restrooms.

"Listen, man, I need time to at least talk to her, and she needs time to talk to her family, put her affairs in order..that sort of thing. As one partner to another, you can at least give us twenty four hours, man, do this one thing for me..I'll owe you one." Blake said desperately never speaking above a whisper. His clothes were drenched with sweat. His thoughts, scrambled and unorganized, failed him when he most needed them.

"You wouldn't be thinking about leaving town now would ya man? You wouldn't do that, I know you wouldn't, I can't believe you'd do that to me.. put me in a spot that way.. you wouldn't, would'ya?" Smith said, pressing his forefinger into Blake's chest,

Blake's mind, racing so fast, he didn't even notice. He thought that if this day ever came he would've been calmer, more collected and certainly better prepared than this. He was losing it, there was too much at stake. Blake leaned against the wall on his back and blew out a long sorrowful breath of air from his lungs. He tried to figure out, how he was going to play this dreadful hand that he'd dealt to himself.

I will never let them take her, he thought. That he knew. He had one card left he could play, but he needed to convince Smith to give him twenty- four hours.

"You got it man." Smith said quietly.

Blake turned to him and asked,

"What time?" he asked looking at his watch.

"It's four thirty, I'll see you tomorrow, same time, in Lou's office. Bring your attorneys, I'm sorry man." And with that he turned and walked away.

Smith's way seemed hard. This had been more difficult than he imagined.

Blake waited until Smith rounded the corner and then he took off for the restaurant.

Evelyn waited anxiously at their usual table. He signaled for her to come over to him. Walking swiftly towards him, hoping that the thing she'd feared the most, hadn't happened. Those beautiful brown eyes looked to him for comfort and protection.

Chapter Nineteen

The office hadn't been anything like it seemed from the outside, room number 216 from outside the door, appeared cold, and unfriendly. Inside, she soon felt comfortable, warm, and secure amongst the huge chenille sofas, funky old lamps, plantation shutters and romantic chandeliers.

Grace sat Evelyn comfortably in the chair and began fitting her with the cast she'd made from a mold prior to her arrival. As soon as it covered her face the lack of air circulation made her face feel sweaty and breathing became mildly labored even with the holes made for her nostrils.

Below, the busy city streets, and its' hum of activity, seemed worlds away, as she went through the discomforting process of changing her identity. Grace Rinsel, a make up artist, originally from London, turned ordinary people into characters most only dreamed of being, agreed to help Evelyn and Blake as a special favor to Mr. Goldstein. Contributing substantial amounts of money each year during their annual fundraising gala, Paul Senior had no problem calling in this much needed favor.

Going further than that, Paul Senior helped Blake plan everything in a matter of three hours.

Offering them his secluded villa in Athens, insisting that due to its' location, they would be safe. When Blake first revealed the plan for escape to Evelyn, she cried, and thought it ludicrous, something out of a mystery novel. Asking her to leave her children, her home, her family and everything familiar to her, she felt she preferred being incarcerated, at least she would be in the states near her children. Secretly she made the decision to turn herself in. But, one important fact stopped her cold. The baby. She kept thinking of her baby being born behind bars, she'd do anything.. anything, not to have that happen. And when Blake pleaded,

"We won't be able to live in this country baby.. but we can live, and we'll be together, all three of us. You don't want the baby to be born behind bars do you? Please honey, they'd take the baby from us." Blake begged. Thinking of her baby, she never considered her idea again.

In a few hours she would be unrecognizable, even to herself. She resigned herself to the fact that her life as she knew it, would be over, nonexistent.

Grace, the best make up artist in Cleveland, worked feverishly to meet the deadline. Most of the prep work, she managed to complete, using a picture sent over earlier by Blake. Coming to this country from England, ten years ago, settling first, in New York City where she thought she would get the experience she needed to master her art. Grace's goal, was to eventually become a noted Hollywood Oscar winning, make-up artist.

Getting very little experience or recognition in New York, she came to Cleveland's theatre district and by a fluke of nature, literally fell into the business of changing the identities of friends in need. Due to her expertise, the underground circulated her name back to Hollywood execs, and in two weeks she'd be leaving for California, where the job of her dreams, awaited her.

So, with her identity completely changed, Evelyn would fly from Cleveland to New York tonight. Arriving in New York La Guardia at eight forty five, she would be led to and secured in a coffin by one of Blake's contacts. Anticipating that if they got off the ground in Cleveland, then Smith, or his contacts would try to apprehend them in New York.

From New York, safe inside the coffin, she would be flown to Greece. If anyone thought of looking inside the coffin, they wouldn't see Evelyn, they would see someone else. She tried not to think of the plan but, it was all she could think of. Unable to bear the thought of being closed up in a coffin, with its' plush bed and pillow, designed to keep the dead comfortable. Blake assured her he'd thought of everything and she'd be perfectly safe. All the questions, such as who would be waiting for her in New York, who would secure her in the coffin, he assured her she didn't have to worry about, she would be approached by one of his people. The coffin, almost guaranteeing her safe passage to Greece, with most officials having no desire to disturb the dead. She had to do it.. remembering that the death angel had shown up unexpectantly in her life, smiling, as he sympathetically prepared to do what he'd been ordered.

With no time for good-byes, and to keep things simple, she wrote letters to everyone, explaining what happened, and to Mike and Lisa, she gave instructions concerning the way she wanted things handled with her children. Mike and Lisa were the only two people she knew could handle her business. There simply wasn't enough time for good-byes, plus saying good-by could put her loved ones in jeopardy. If they knew nothing then they could tell nothing.

She'd made things simple, by dividing the money into two accounts, one account for Devon and one for Sissy. Mike would make sure the money was used for their education and to keep up the taxes on the house. The rest she'd transferred into an off shore account under an assumed name.

For those fleeting moments, when she considered changing her mind, she looked down at the red boots she wore, reminding herself that it was okay, she only did it to keep her daughter alive. She could still see her, bending down in her closet looking for the red boots, a beautiful smile on her face and she thought to herself, I wouldn't change a thing.

Grace maneuvered around the chair putting on the final touches of make-up, on a new face which now belonged to her. Next, the hair, which sat still and lifeless atop the wig stand, waiting to assume the identity of it's new owner, being carefully sewn onto her hair.

A new passport arrived by messenger. The name on the passport read Juanita Walker. Evelyn knew that it was the name of Blake's deceased grandmother. But the woman in the photo wasn't Blake's grandmother, it was Evelyn. Not the old Evelyn, but the new Evelyn whose picture now graced the passport photo, posed for by the stranger in a melancholy way, as if it were the millionth time she'd posed.

She would not see Blake again until she arrived in Greece, and took a cab to the address he'd given her. Grace informed her, she would not go back to her car, Grace would take her to the airport; her plane was scheduled to leave in two hours.

"I know that you're nervous but trust me everything has been well planned and, from what little I know about your situation, you had very few options available to you. Blake really loves you. I've known him for five years now and I've never seen him as happy as he has been lately.. I want to see you two stay together. Now you can sit up.. I need to do your hair now, we're running out of time." Grace said.

Evelyn sat up quickly but purposely avoided looking in the mirror that hung on the wall directly in front of her. Wanting to delay seeing herself having been changed into the stranger in the photo, she could wait a bit longer. Grace went over to the wig stand and removed the hair,

"Come with me." Grace directed. Evelyn jumped down from the reclining chair and followed Grace into the salon area. Mirrors lined one wall and two stylist chairs sat in front of the mirrors. One lone dryer sat over in the corner next to a shampoo bowl. Grace motioned for her to sit in the first stylist chair and she unfolded the hair. Behind her on a tray lay the implements she needed to weave in the hair. She picked up the big arched needle and beginning in Evelyn's nape area she made the first hook. She then took the hair, unraveled the hair and she began measuring the first braid in her nape area. After cutting the weft she began sewing the hair onto Evelyn's braided hair, using the hook and the braid as her foundation. The bang part of her hair was left free and blended in with the weaved hair. When Grace finished curling and styling the hair you could not tell that it was a hair weave. The finished product was an uncanny duplicate of the style worn by the stranger in the passport photo.

"Take a look, sweety." Grace turned Evelyn around so that she could look in the mirror at the new stranger called, Juanita Walker. Juanita was an older lady in her fifty's or sixty's and she was about thirty pounds heavier than Evelyn. Evelyn panicked, her slender body didn't match the heavier body in the photo.

"Not to worry.. we're not finished yet..over here sweety." Grace said politely pointing to a fitting room around the corner filled with naked mannequins and generic face molds, eerily standing in various poises, some with lips parted as if about to speak.

"Take off your clothes and put this on, you've got exactly fifteen minutes. We need an hour to get to the airport." She ended pulling the curtain giving Evelyn her privacy. Evelyn did as she was told. Holding the foam body suit in her hand, she stared at it thankful it would add the extra thirty or so pounds she needed. Fighting back the tears as she began removing the clothes from the rack, thinking, this is real, I can't turn back now, she resolved.

Totally outfitted, she stepped in front of the mirror she couldn't believe how much she resembled the woman in the photo, the word amazing, was inadequate. Grace was a genius.

In a navy blue woman's pant suit, red and white blouse, navy tame and the treasured red suede boots, to remind her of Sissy, Juanita Walker, was well put together. Evelyn thanked Grace, giving her a big hug. They left hurriedly for the airport.

Arriving at the ariport, realizing only she had the ability to hold up her part of the plan, Evelyn felt the tears forming in her eyes again. She fought to hold them back as she existed the car, not wanting to attract any unwanted attention.

"How can I ever thank you, you saved my life,"she said to Grace.

"It's all good girl. If it's a girl, name her Grace.. good bye, Evelyn see you on the big screen." With that she pulled off, leaving Evelyn overwhelmed with feelings of abandonment.

She was on her own. Feeling disconnected from the busy crowd, every body and everything she held dear in the world. There she stood, bewildered and alone. Soon she would be a hunted woman for the murder of her daughter's lover. She didn't think she could ever sink any lower than that.

Having been provided a boarding pass she had no bags to check, didn't need to go to the ticket counter. Her boarding pass read, Gate B- eleven. Her plane was due to depart in forty- five minutes exactly.

The activity in the airport was hurried and chaotic. Heading home after the Christmas holidays, passengers were running on top of each other, in hurried disarray to meet their departing flights. She passed through the security gate with no trouble at all but the real test would come in New York. Her stomach flip-flopped at the very thought of it. She thought about the woman in the passport photo and wondered who was the stranger, and why had she gotten herself involved in her troubles. One thing for sure Evelyn thought, if that woman was brave enough to help her, then she had to be brave enough to help herself. She wondered though, if going to prison for what she'd done hadn't been the right thing to do. She had always been taught that paying your debt to society is what God expected of you.

Picking up the pace, she hurried further down the airport corridor, anxious to get to her gate, find a seat and rest. Lately, she was always tired and sleepy. Once they settled in Athens, assuming she made it safely, she would find a doctor immediately and have her pregnancy confirmed. At her age pregnancy was a matter for concern. *Men never thought about anything but what they wanted*, she thought.

Evelyn found the gate, double checked her ticket, and sat down heavily. She missed Blake and wondered where he was. At the last minute, he'd phoned Grace to say they would be on the same flight after all, making her feel safer. They came separately, just in case Smith had somebody watching them and the odds were, he did. Evelyn scanned the crowd of passengers seated in her gate area. Blake definitely wasn't there.

"Ladies and gentleman flight seven thirty seven to New York LaGuardia, is now ready for boarding. Passengers with special needs can come forward to be seated." Two people pushed by attendants were wheeled to the ramp, disappearing inside. "Those passengers flying first class may come forward and present their boarding passes for boarding." The attendant announced. The first class passengers stood, rushing and pushing their way over to the young man that would take their boarding passes, feeding them into an automated machine. Evelyn looked around again to see if she saw Blake anywhere. Probably disguised, if she saw him, she might not be able to recognize him.

Some people still waited in line to receive their boarding passes. Evelyn looked again, closely. The first woman in line, a Mexican.. no she didn't think so.. too short. The next person in line, a white man in golf attire, golf clubs sat on the floor beside his feet. Evelyn studied his hands and his hair carefully, she couldn't be sure. Openly staring at him, he finally turned, returning her stare. Nope, definitely not, it wasn't Blake, too skinny. They had ways of adding pounds to you but taking pounds off in a matter of hours, Evelyn couldn't see how that could be possible. Next in line, a tall, big-boned black woman. Her hair, braided into a shoulder length bob that partially covered her left eye. Her gaze slowly took in the woman's hands..it was him, she could recognize Blake's hands anywhere. Complete with fake, red press on nails, makeup and boobs, had she not been carefully searching for him, she would never have known it was him, it was a helluva job. Making eye contact quickly, being careful not to linger, just in case someone was watching, she felt better just knowing he was with her.

"We will now seat rows eleven through eighteen." The flight attendant announced.

Evelyn got up slowly thanking God all the way that she and Blake were still free and still together. Taking the seat by the window as her ticket indicated, she saw Blake seating himself four rows ahead of her. This way he'd be discovered first, distracting anyone who came looking for them.

Travelers continued to pile onto the plane, looking for their seats numbers, removing their coats and placing luggage in the storage bin above the seats. A young white girl and her fiancée took the seats next to Evelyn . After the last passenger came aboard and the stewardess began the final lock down for take off, Evelyn settled comfortably into her seat. She watched through the window as the workers loaded the luggage into the belly of the plane. It was a beautiful day for flying, with the sky a brilliant blue, a hint that the sun hung happily somewhere beyond the puffs of the soft white clouds ,brought immeasurable comfort to her as she thought about the new land she would soon occupy.

Deep in thought, she was slow to realize, that the take off had been abruptly aborted by a commotion at the front door. The stewardess ran up the aisle and whispered something to her co-worker. Evelyn couldn't read her lips. They both went to the front entrance of the plane above the first class passengers. They stood in a huddle, speaking urgently, but too softly for her to hear. Finally, the pilot appeared and instructed them to open the door to the plane. Passengers began talking amongst themselves, wondering what the problem could be as the closed entry door was reopened.

As if looking at a movie, standing outside of her body, the unthinkable happened. As if he were in her dream, Detective Smith appeared, looming as tall as a giant in the tiny arched, entranceway to the plane. Evelyn thought that it was surely over now, but she would fight until the end. Opening her bag, she took out her crochet needle and a ball of yarn that she always carried with her. Concentrating on making the first loop, in order to steady her shaking hands, Evelyn kept her head down, not too low, not too high in an effort to appear indifferent, giving Smith no reason for his gaze to linger on her. She looked up sporadically in an effort to appear normal.

All the passengers had been seated and buckled in, in preparation for take off. Only one empty seat remained. Smith's attention landed immediately on the empty seat,

"I thought I told you not to let any of the passengers move for any reason. Who was sitting here?" Smith said, annoyed, pointing to the empty seat, with shaking hands, angry at his own stupidity for trusting Blake Shaking too, from the exasperation he felt, having the entire precinct know he was a whistle blower, yet couldn't produce the prisoner. He was more than desperate to recover Blake and Evelyn, his integrity was hanging in the balance.

At Lou's insistence, two officers from the precinct reluctantly accompanied him, they waited outside the plane, covering the ground. Another officer stood watch at the back of the plane.

"Officer we really can't be sure exactly who was sitting in that seat but if you'll give us a few minutes, we can certainly find out. However, I did notice that the restroom is occupied and I believe that the person occupying the empty seat is in there." The stewardess said nervously, trying to pacify Smith.

"You two, get into your seats and stay there until I say different." Smith rudely ordered the stewardesses. The stewardesses scurried back to their fold down seats, that faced the passengers. With that the pilot who had been watching from the door of the cockpit turned around and took his seat as his co pilot continued to prepare the plane for take off.

Smith began a slow, methodical descent down the aisle, carefully inspecting each row more importantly the faces and eyes in each row, sniffing with the precision of a hungry rat. The urge to urinate came flooding down into Evelyn's abdomen. The powerful rush of fluid splashed angrily against the walls of her frightened bladder. She tightened her vaginal muscles, pushed her legs together and prayed to the good Lord, he was her only hope.

Blake covered his hands with the shawl he carried, he pulled out his organizer and busied himself with that. When Smith reached Evelyn's row, the young girl's fiancé, growing increasingly agitated, blurted out,

"Officer, you do have a search warrant, don't you? You can't search us without one you know." The rebellious young man said as he ran his fingers through his curly red hair. Smith narrowed his eyes and replied indignantly,

"Listen you..you had better keep your shirt on pal and hope that I don't run you in for interfering with a police investigation." Smith said bitterly. The young girl nudged her fiancée and reluctantly, he quieted down.

When Smith finished his inspection of each row he turned his attention to the passenger in the rest room. His partner had been posted there during his entire search. Cautiously approaching the door, he motioned for his partner to come up front exchanging positions with him. Smith prudently placed his ear to the door of the bathroom and listened intently for a minute. He then knocked, as all of the passengers turned attentively around in their seats. Getting no response he knocked harder and harder, his knock turning into loud beating and banging. When that failed to yield him any results, he yelled,

"This is Detective Smith from the Police Department, this plane has been seized and is under investigation. I need you to step outside of the rest room immediately, or else we're coming in. Come out now!" Smith spoke to the door, easing his revolver from its holster. Passengers gasped, some begin screaming and others hit the floor, thinking the exchange of gunfire was imminent.

Smith stepped back to allow the door clearance when it opened. Still, when the door opened it slammed into his nose, blood spurted from his nostrils.

"Jeeesus, Christ!" Smith yelled, jumping back even farther, grabbing his throbbing nose. He pulled out his handkerchief and dabbed at the blood that began to ooze. By this time the climate inside the plane was one of utter chaos, with everyone afraid of getting shot.

Evelyn secretly thanked God for the person in the restroom, who'd caused the distraction. When everybody finally got a good look at the person behind the door, they all smiled. Stepping away from the door, a kindly, old white lady, hobbling along on shaky legs, slowly existed the restroom. Hearing impaired , she sauntered down the aisle, unaware of the commotion she'd caused by being absent from her seat.

"I suppose that's the fugitive, eh." The red headed young man with a British accent, quietly poked fun at Smith. Detective Smith stalked off the plane in abject defeat, rudely brushing past his partner and stomping off the plane in a child like manner.

Outside he ordered his partners to continue the search and they all swiftly moved in different directions, leaving Smith behind to mentally kick himself in the butt for letting Blake slip through his hands. Evelyn picked up her crotchet needle and began stitching a blanket for her unborn child.

Sissy- Years Later

Sissy turned the key to her office, unlocked the door, and went inside. The aroma of french roasted coffee, told her that Auntie Lee Lee was already there working. Sissy took her coat off and hung it in the closet beside her office. Auntie Lee Lee, busy freshening up the examining rooms, hummed the jazz tune that played over the intercom system Jimmy and Devon installed, just last month. She thought about her husband, Jimmy, and felt that tickling sensation in the pit of her stomach, still.

When she'd finished her undergrad work at Tuskegee, she'd married Jimmy who by then had already finished two years of law school. Agreeing on their wedding day not to get pregnant until Sissy finished medical school, to their dismay she got pregnant with little Jimmy on their honeymoon. Thank God for Jimmy's mother, Miss Hazel who jumped right in and helped with the children, enabling them both to pursue their careers. After little Jimmy, came her daughter Niteria and then her baby boy, Lamont.

None of this would've been possible had it not been for the sacrifices made by her beloved mother. Sissy closed her eyes and pictured her face. She pictured herself as a youngster being picked up and held to her mother's bosom, feeling the vibration of her laughter on her cheeks. Missing her mother's arms around her left a void in her life that would be forever present. Nobody's arms felt like her mothers, strong but soft, firm yet tender, correcting but fair.

It amazed her, the lengths her mother went to in order to save her life. And save her life she did. Giving up her freedom and her life so that she could live without fearing, that at any moment, her life may be ended. She imagined her mother escaping by boat or plane, whichever, running for her life, ducking and dodging, perhaps frightened yet deteermined.

Nobody knew the extent of abuse she had suffered. Sometimes being held at gunpoint to keep Brandon from hurting her family. Sissy hadn't expected that she would live to go to college, hadn't expected anything good to happen to her, while Brandon held her in a sort of prison.. prison of the body and prison of the mind.

It wasn't a surprise to anyone that nothing good ever came of the Jones' family, with Mrs. Jones dying a few years back from liver failure, and Brandon's little brother Jason, receiving life, for stabbing his girlfriend to death. Their entire family had been wiped out.

The outer office door opened, breaking into Sissy's thoughts, indicating that her first patient had arrived and her day was officially beginning. Auntie Lee Lee greeted the first patient, Mrs. Livingston and her baby, Justin.

"Well now how is the big man today, huh? Justin, I hear you've kept Mom up all night with that fever, huh?" Auntie Lee Lee said, pulling Justin's chart and heading for an examination room, "let's get you undressed, big man." she said to Mrs.Livingston. The phone rang and Sissy picked it up on her way to her office. She needed to comb her hair and put on a little makeup and find her lab jacket.

Auntie Lee Lee had stepped into her life, as Evelyn requested. Wearing Evelyn's shoes, still unable to fill them, but Sissy adored her for trying so hard. She and Uncle Mike had seen to it that everything went on just as if her mother and father were here. They attended everything she and Devon were involved in.

When Sissy began plans to open her office, Auntie Lee Lee insisted that she would work there for free for the first year, after which Sissy could put her on salary. It had turned out to be the best arrangement ever. It got Auntie Lee Lee out of the house and back practicing nursing and it saved money that Sissy and Jimmy didn't have at the time. Sissy's pediatric practice eventually took off and when the year was up she paid Auntie Lee Lee a good salary, plus perks, she was worth every dime and more.

"Good morning Dr. Lyon's office." Sissy answered as she went over little Justin's symptoms in her head.

"Good morning Dr. Lyons, I'm calling for your brother Mr. Hill. I'll put you on hold and he'll pick up the extension." Devon's secretary, Gloria informed her. "Thank You, Gloria." Sissy responded wondering what her brother could want this early in the morning. She and Devon had become inseparable since their mother had fled the country. Finally, Devon's voice came over the phone line,

"Hey Sis, I got the tickets," He said trying to keep the excitement in his voice from showing. Sissy squealed with excitement,

"So we're really going? Does she know," Sissy asked excitedly.

"No, I thought we'd just call her when we got to the airport." Devon teased.

"Now you have to give her more notice than that, bro." Sissy insisted.

"I know, I'm just teasing you girl. Let everybody know and for God's sake start your packing now Sissy. I don't want to miss the flight. Okay gotta go, I'm due in court in twenty minutes, later." Her brother hung up quickly.

Sissy thought about what she'd do when she first saw her mother. She wondered how her mother looked, how aging had changed her appearance. She hung up the phone and walked slowly to her office, sat down at her desk and pulled it out. Usually reading it once each month, today she felt the need to read it.

It was the last piece of correspondence between her and her mother, the day she disappeared from their lives. She kept the letter and when feeling particularly lonely for her, she would get the letter out, always feeling better after reading it. She removed it from the plastic folder she kept it in and unfolded it. She held the letter to her face and inhaled her mother's scent, which surprisingly, she could still smell. Then she began to read her mother's letter, which after all these years of reading it, she'd memorized, word for word,

Dear Precious One,

As I write you this letter in haste, I can see your face in my mind, the face that you have now and the many faces from the different stages of development that I've seen your face evolve into. I've loved every single one of those faces, and I cherish every moment I spent looking at them. Not being able to look at you as you develop into a woman is what will hurt the most. But I made the decision that I wanted you to live to develop into a woman and to achieve your dreams, no matter what the cost.

I've done something of which I am not proud. Still, truthfully speaking, as a mother I realize now that I can be ruthless when it comes to your happiness and well being. I am happy to suffer any kind of consequence for my actions, if it means that you will enjoy a decent quality of life. I will not try to justify what I have done, other than to say, that something inside of me would not allow me to stand by and watch your life be snuffed out for no reason. I was aware of everything that happened, which brought me to the conclusion I came to, to end his life, and darling let me just say to you, you are the bravest person I know. Truly, you are my hero, the way you tried to save us, by offering up your own life to save ours. I knew that I'd raised an exceptional human being, but I never had a clue that I raised a young lady with such depth of character.

As God is my witness if I'd had any other options available to me then, I wouldn't be writing this letter.

Mommy needs for you to promise her something in my absence. I need you to put this horrible situation behind you and bury it. Promise me that you will never,

ever think that in anyway you brought this upon the family. Leave the blame where it should be, at the feet of Brandon Jones. Please, don't ever think that there must have been something wrong with you or else you wouldn't have gotten involved with such a character. Instead, when you arise each morning I want you to look into the mirror and say to yourself, what a blessed person I am, my mother loved me so very much, she was happy, and sweetheart I do mean happy, to give up my freedom so that you would have certain liberties in life.

Remember this sweetheart, it is a pledge I made to you the day they placed you in my arms when you were born, to love you deeper than the ocean floor, to lift you higher than the heavens, I will do anything for you, I will go anywhere on your behalf, to guarantee your well being and to speak only good and lovely things that bring life into your soul, and joy into your heart, you are my baby. No matter how old you get people will always refer to you as Evelyn's baby, remember that.

And so, my precious, one thing I need for you to do is to go on out there and live your life with vigor, for me, you must laugh, you must cry, you must yell, you must scream and most importantly, you must love. And When you find your husband, you must make lots of love and when the babies come, they must receive double the kisses, kisses from you and kisses from me.

Tell them about me. Tell them that their grandma had to leave, because she needed their mother to have them. My arms are empty where you and your babies should be. My heart feels lonely because you aren't here to speak to it. When I had you Sissy, God gave me the best, when I'd done nothing to deserve such a gift, but every since that day, I've felt it an honor and did the best I knew how with such greatness he'd bestowed upon me. The memory of our last kiss and hug lingers in my mind and I will hold on to it as tightly and for as long I can, postponing the moment when it will fade from my memory, but not my heart.

I do not want you to grieve for me because then the sacrifice I made would then be in vain, realizing that I truly count it all joy to have found myself in a position to help you, my beloved. So, please, my precious one, go on out there and kick butt. You must always stay with your brother, I want the two of you to stay together. He loves you like no other and as the head of our house now, I too must accept his covering and words of wisdom he speaks into our lives.

Sissy, I saved the most important message for last. I pray that you will return to God. You are an adult now and must give an account for yourself. I feel that somehow our family became too complacent, having been so blessed, we became consumed by the things of the world and our God is a jealous God, he will have no other God before him. Return to him, you and Devon and sweetheart I can then rest in peace knowing that your footsteps from this day forward will be ordered by Him.

I will get another message to you through Auntie Lee Lee and Uncle Mike as soon as I am able.

Loving You Forever,
Mommy

Sissy folded the letter and placed in back into it's plastic cover and realized she'd never really known her mother at all. She was a phenomenal woman and if she could just be half the woman her mother was, she would feel she'd done something great.

After almost ten years absence, it became clear to them that Evelyn had no intentions of ever coming back to the states, she loved her life there in Athens, Greece. Sissy sat daydreaming about the visit. Seeing her mother, Blake and her brothers made her tremble with excitement. Everybody was going, even Auntie Lee Lee and Uncle Mike. It would be some reunion.

The reunion- Evelyn

Evelyn busied herself making a final inspection of the dinner table she'd set for her family. Then she inspected herself by looking into the old mirror she'd picked up at the flea market in town. Maybe her heart would begin to heal now that she was going to see her children, grandchildren, her family and her dear friends Mike and Lisa. Her face hadn't changed much except for the beginnings of little crow's feet at the corner of her eyes. Still she checked it again in the mirror from all angles, wondering what everybody would think of her appearance. She was nervous and she didn't know why. She had gained fifteen pounds after the birth of the twins but she was comfortable with that. Instead of being a perfect size eight, she now wore a size ten. A couple of gray strands of hair had surfaced in her temple area, but gave her a distinguished appearance. All in all the trauma she had sustained in her life had been kind enough not to show up on her body and ruin her looks, looking pretty much as she did when living in the states. But even if her appearance remained the same, she wasn't the same. That explained her nervousness. She was different, made different by the love of God, who now lived inside her. She hoped she'd be able to share this with the people she loved the most in the world, her family.

Her son Trevor ran into the room.

"Mommy? What time is our cousins coming?" he said, his good looks always weakening her resolve.

"Slow down young man. Remember to walk when you're in the house, not run. Now, for the tenth time, they are not your cousins that are coming, they are your brother and sister, remember? Now, you and your brother go and wash up and change your clothes, it's almost time for us to leave for the airport." Evelyn instructed her son. He turned and ran towards his bedroom yelling to his twin brother,

"Waymond..Waymond, it's time, it's time to go to the airport and pick up our cousins..I mean our brotter. Mommy say, wash up and change, git'cho clothes on, and I'm first!" Evelyn heard them both scurrying towards the bathroom.

What a blessing they'd turned out to be. When the doctor first told her that she was having twins she had cried. She felt that it was too much drama for her after what she'd been through. Blake had been ecstatic about having twins and immediately built a new house in preparation for their arrival. That was ten years ago and Evelyn hardly remembered the two o'clock feedings and diaper changes.

Blake kept busy with his private investigation business and Evelyn opened up an interior design school that kept her quite busy. Evelyn loved Athens with it's scenic countryside, beautiful landscapes and historic landmarks, she was here to stay.

"Where are the boys? We need to get started baby." Blake announced as he breezed past her and headed for the shower. They had both worked hard around the house getting it ready for the arrival of the family, acting as if they were expecting royalty. Evelyn heard Blake turn on the shower in their bathroom and begin to hum to himself. He'd made a good husband, most women weren't blessed to have two good husbands in one lifetime, but God have given her favor in that way.

Evelyn went back to the kitchen and did yet another last minute check. She needed to chill, she was freakin' just thinking about seeing her family. Everything was as it should be, the greens were humming and she'd made her famous macaroni and cheese. Her roast beef was so tender until it almost melted on your tongue. Of course she had fixed turkey and dressing , loaded with fresh portabello mushrooms. Potato salad, candied yams, ham and for dessert peach cobbler and chocolate cake. The favorite dishes of all of her loved ones had been carefully and lovingly prepared. Evelyn set the oven on warm and went to the pantry to get her ice chest. She put the two bags of ice Blake bought into the chest and put a few canned pops on ice to chill. The table in the dinning room needed fresh flowers on it so she went outside and pulled some beautiful wild flowers. Outside it was sunny and humid , perfect for a family reunion. After dinner they'd all go outside and watch the sunset, there were none prettier anywhere else in the world.

Evelyn often thought of different ways she should have handled her daughter's abusive lover but when she was going through it nothing seemed normal to her. Keeping her daughter alive felt to her like a natural part of being a mother.

She often dreamed of Sissy and her life as it is now. The good part being, that Sissy had a life. She watched the videotapes Sissy sent her of her marriage, graduation and the birth of her grandchildren. Evelyn sometimes spent entire weekends watching those tapes and crying tears of happiness. Never would she treat life casually again. Every moment was treasured and treated with respect.

"It's time to go Mommy." The twins chimed together, as they jumped into the van Blake had rented to accommodate the big crowd that would be arriving shortly. As Blake pulled out onto the road Evelyn smiled as the warm breeze covered her face.

About the Author

Vanessa Collier lives in Ohio with her husband and two children. A Mother's Solution, truly a labor of love, is her first novel- Dedicated and passionate about giving a voice to the victims of domestic violence who mostly suffer in silence, from this number one killer of African American women.

Vanessa is an educator, currently working on her next novel. She attended Ashland University, where she received her M.Ed. in educational administration. Recently, having been inducted into Who's Who Among America's Teachers Vanessa works hard to keep her students encouraged and achieving their goals.

Vanessa would love to hear from women readers interested in stopping the violence against women, or if you would like her to speak to your group please contact her at this email address: van50c@aol.com

Printed in the United States
40023LVS00001B/121-147

9 781420 852035